Stories for
a Lost Child

AMERICAN INDIAN STUDIES SERIES

Stories for a Lost Child

Carter Meland

To ALLISON
STEP LONG, LIVE TALL!

Cat Meland
#mmiw

MICHIGAN STATE UNIVERSITY PRESS | *East Lansing*

⊛ The paper used in this publication meets the minimum requirements
of ANSI/NISO z39.48-1992 (R 1997) (Permanence of Paper).

Michigan State University Press
East Lansing, Michigan 48823-5245

Printed and bound in the United States of America.

26   25   24   23   22   21   20   19   18   17   1   2   3   4   5   6   7   8   9   10

LIBRARY OF CONGRESS CATALOGING-IN-PUBLICATION DATA
Names: Meland, Carter author.
Title: Stories for a lost child / Carter Meland.
Description: East Lansing : Michigan State University Press, 2017. | Series: American Indian studies series
Identifiers: LCCN 2016027760 | ISBN 9781611862447 (pbk. : alk. paper) | ISBN 9781609175269 (pdf)
| ISBN 9781628952964 (epub) | ISBN 9781628962963 (kindle)
Classification: LCC PS3613.E44443 A6 2016 | DDC 813/.6—dc23
LC record available at https://lccn.loc.gov/2016027760

Book design by Charlie Sharp, Sharp Des!gns, East Lansing, Michigan
Cover design by Erin Kirk New
Cover image: James D. Autio, *Ahab*. ©2012. Digital manipulation of acrylic and gesso
on journal cover, 5½" × 8¾". Personal collection of Beth Copeland.

Michigan State University Press is a member of the Green Press Initiative and is
committed to developing and encouraging ecologically responsible publishing
practices. For more information about the Green Press Initiative and the use
of recycled paper in book publishing, please visit *www.greenpressinitiative.org.*

Visit Michigan State University Press at *www.msupress.org*

To Sally
~ for giving me the time ~

To Will and Liv
~ for making the most of it ~

PART ONE

Inside the Box

Before Fiona could stop him, Strep opened the box and pulled out its contents. He stood on the top step of her house, the postal service box in one hand and a sheaf of papers in the other. "Couldn't you just wait a minute?" she said. "You said it was addressed to me."

"I thought it would be full of cool stuff," Strep said, his wide smile fading to a dim look of puzzled disappointment. "Gifts, candy, a video game—something useful, you know."

Fiona knew he meant something that would add some kind of spark to their summer vacation. The dog days of August were nearing, and their break from school had lost some of its luster. They had spent the early part of the afternoon at Dane's, shooting hoops, but the game dragged as the heat intensified.

"It's nothing but paper, Fee." As he flapped the stack of papers in front of her, two envelopes fluttered out from beneath the rubber band that held the bundle together. "And they're all just covered in writing." He riffled the pages with his thumb. "Maybe it's the world's longest letter?" The stack was as thick as a book.

Fiona looked at the two envelopes that had fluttered down on the step. Her name was written on one, while the other had landed upside down.

"Didn't this guy ever hear of e-mail or FaceTime?" Strep was still puzzled about the pages and pages of writing in his hand. "There's lots easier ways to tell you something than writing." He glanced at the top page. "Blackbird Coffee," he read and turned to Fiona. "I wonder what that means."

Fiona shrugged her shoulders, and while she retrieved the fallen envelopes, Strep began to read to her.

I don't speak Anishinaabemowin, the language of our Anishinaabe ancestors, but I know a few words, and the words I know may once have made me invisible. On the other hand, it may have been bird magic that transformed me for those few seconds. Either way I disappeared. Here's what happened:

I went into one of those big suburban malls to get a jar of instant coffee at the dollar store. Inside the mall there was a blackbird darting from perch to perch above the courtyard, disoriented by the skylights that showed the outdoors while prohibiting it. Settled for a moment, the bird showed me its profile, glancing at me sidewise and yellow-eyed.

When I was a little boy, your great-grandfather told me that if I wanted to communicate with deer, I had to speak to them in Anishinaabemowin, the language of the woodland. Recalling this as I looked at the bird, I manufactured something respectful—I hoped—out of the handful of words I was familiar with.

Trusting the creature's sharp senses, I looked up at him and spoke under my breath, "*Boozhoo, makade-mashkikiwaaboo.*" I hoped the black-feathered sky-surveyor would see the aptness in being addressed as the black hot liquid I mix up out of a jar.

Inspired by my attention;

startled by my ability to haltingly speak in a comprehensible language;

and/or offended by my words, the bird took wing and became liquid for a moment, a black dash across a white ceiling. Drawn by the blue earthlight dropping through the sky holes above, the bird sped into the deceptive glass and spilled to the floor twenty feet away.

With the words still warm in my mouth, I moved toward the fallen animal. Lifting the bird in my hands and stepping toward the exit I became immune to the stares of shoppers and window washers. No one could see me. Moments later I was outside, kneeling by a shrub near the entrance, the bird at rest in the shade.

A few days later I had a dream: I'm watching the security tape in a dark room. I see myself turn toward the sky, move my lips, take seven steps, and disappear.

Strep had stumbled over some of the unfamiliar words in the story—*Anishinaabe, boozhoo, makade-mashkikiwaaboo*—but still managed to finish.

He looked at Fiona. "I don't get it," he said. "Did the bird die?"

Uncertain herself, Fiona shook her head. "I don't know." She looked at the envelopes in her hand. Both were quite thick, each bulging from the papers folded up inside them. The flap on the upside down one was even taped shut, like the envelope had to be forced to hold whatever was inside it. Flipping it over, she saw it was addressed "To: the Grandchild." She wasn't sure exactly what that meant and hoped that the one addressed to "Fiona" might explain it.

Opening the "Fiona" envelope, she took out the bundle of pages and scanned the first one. "It says these are stories from my Indian grandpa." Fiona tipped the letter toward Strep and lowered herself to the step.

Strep settled next to her. "Your mom's dad, right?"

Fiona nodded, afraid of what she might say in response to Strep. She loved her mom but didn't want him to know that she only mostly loved her. She loved her dad, their home, her friends, and, in all, her life—but there was a hole there, too, in her life, one her mom refused to fill and only ever barely acknowledged. Her grandpa. The Indian.

"If I ask about him, just about all she ever says is, 'Your grandma and I were better off without him.'" Fiona let her voice fall flat just as her mom did when she said those words. Emotionless, she looked into the distance over Strep's shoulder as she spoke, rather than in his eyes. Imitating her mom, who always acted like she was wished she were dead in those rare moments when she mentioned him. She always acted like she was alone then, too, even with her daughter right there. When she was younger, Fiona had tried yelling at her, shouting that she wasn't being fair, that she needed to tell her about her grandfather. "Tell me who he was!" she shouted. "Tell me why you were better off. Tell me something!" Words like that still stormed through her head whenever Mom dismissed her questions, but Fiona held them back now. She knew if she let them loose, Mom would only nervously laugh—quietly, but sort of scornfully as well—and walk away, still unable to look her daughter in the eye. The first time Mom had walked away like that was after she refused to tell Fiona what tribe Grandpa was—what tribe they were!—and unsure of what to do, Fiona had dashed down the basement and smashed her arm against the cold concrete floor again and again and again, hoping to break her wrist so it would shatter just the way her heart felt. That shattered wrist would punish her mom for not saying anything. It would show her to take her daughter's questions seriously. She hadn't even managed to raise a bruise before her fury was spent.

After that, she started retreating to her room at those moments, frustrated and exasperated. For a while punching her pillow had worked in settling her anger, as did crying, but then they stopped working. Slipping on her headphones and listening to her music had never worked. Everything seemed like a meaningless gesture that only left her feeling more empty.

Still, the closed door of her room was the best barrier against all aggravation. Just the quiet was good. She tried reading behind it sometimes. Books offered consolation in other situations, but this family thing was different. Lately, she'd tried filling her phone with pages of notes that she always deleted. She was unsure if it was the writing or the deleting that left her feeling more settled, but it was something.

Not even realizing what was going on in her mind, Strep chuckled at Fiona's imitation of her mom. "Sometimes it's scary how much you look like her, Fee."

"Don't say that, Strep." Even more than everyone else, Strep towered over her, even sitting down. She looked up at him. "Believe me, that's not a good thing at this moment." She never wanted to have that blank look of her mother's and that reluctance to speak about things, even if they hurt. There was something that Mom thought she'd put behind her, but it seemed to Fiona that she'd only hidden it away. If it were behind her, she would be able tell Fiona anything she wanted to know.

"It's not in a bad way, Fee." Strep stumbled around the words a second. "My mom says you are both 'sweet and petite.'"

"If she were all that sweet, mom would tell me something about him, wouldn't she?" Fiona felt her jaw tighten; the frustration again. "She doesn't give anything away when she talks about him, you know? Just 'We were better off without him.' Just flat and unemotional, like she was talking about a dog that ran away, not her dad. It makes me so angry." Fiona felt the sting of tears rising and bowed her head toward the letter.

She felt his hand tentatively, awkwardly pat her shoulder. "You seem more sad than mad, Fee."

Looking up at him again, seeing the concern in his eyes, she was tempted to lean into him and let everything spill. How her mother's silence hurt, because for all her concern and all her care, mom just kept the past to herself—but it was their past, not just hers. She wanted to tell him that looking even slightly different from most everyone in their suburban cul-de-sac world was weird, unsettling, and if Mom would talk about who they were, it might help her feel less lost. Strep knew her so well he didn't even see it anymore, but her dusky skin was a stark contrast to the acres of pink in the locker room after gym class, meaning she was a stark contrast to those girls with the bobbing blonde ponytails sprouting from the tops of their heads. Though she had plenty of friends, she wanted to tell him that she always felt a bit like E.T. in that old movie. Someone from elsewhere. Where, though, is what she needed to know. The question made her angry and sad and sometimes it just wore her out because she felt like she'd used up all the different ways she could think of to get Mom to answer it.

"I'm still stuck on that bird," Strep said. "It flies into the glass up there and falls to the floor. He picks it up and then he disappears."

Fiona smiled weakly. Strep was trying to get her to think about her grandfather, not her mom. Like all the boys his age, he was so easy to see through. Sweet and—what was a good word, for it? Unsophisticated. Boys. None of them were subtle, but then neither was her mom, really. Mom thought she'd kept her father hidden from the family, but Fiona had found something that showed he had not disappeared from their lives as much as Mom pretended.

"I found out a little something about him a couple years ago." Fiona looked up from the letter resting on her knee.

"About who, the bird?" Strep grinned.

Fiona shook her head. He was such a dork; he knew she meant her grandpa. Boys. "It's something Mom never shared with me."

"About your grandpa," Strep stated as if he didn't know.

"Yes, about my grandpa. Who was an Indian. Who wrote these stories." Fiona tapped the bundle of papers on Strep's knee and then playfully punched his arm in mock frustration. "Dang, can you just stop for a second so I can tell you what I found?"

Sometimes these unsophisticated boys knew how to make her feel better. Strep's easy humor, while not always witty or profound, was classic in ways that she, like pretty much everyone else, found endearing.

"You said you found him. I already know."

"Stop." Fiona punched him again. "Do you want to hear or not?"

Strep, grinning, nodded his head too eagerly, a puppy panting at the thought of a game of fetch.

"I said stop, Strep. This is serious."

"Sorry, Fee. I'll try to behave."

"I've never told anyone about this, so if you want to hear you got to promise not to let it slip." Fiona looked up at him sternly.

"Sounds mysterious," he said. "This better be good."

"It's probably not all that exciting, but I never knew about it before, and Mom still doesn't know I know."

Strep leaned in closer. "I'm ready," he said. No grin. No jokes.

"I was snooping around in my mom's dresser drawer a couple years ago—"

"You do that, too? My mom always stashes extra cash there and sometimes a guy just needs a pastry or a donut—or both." He smiled.

"My mom does the same, and I was looking for some money to get a pop when I came across an old photo."

"Black and white, I bet."

"It was—a shot of my grandma and grandpa. He was in a suit and she was in this nice white dress. I thought it looked like a wedding picture even though it didn't look like those formal, churchy ones all our parents have. Her dress was more simple than those elaborate gowns. When I turned it over I saw I was right." Fiona smiled, recalling the words there: "Robinson and I, with the Justice of the Peace, August 1, 1964" was penciled on the back in a curling, elegant cursive. Her grandma's handwriting. "Mom had never shown it to me," she said and then told Strep how the justice of the peace stood between her grandma and grandpa in the picture, and all three were beaming for the photographer. "It looked like Grandpa had just finished saying something that made the justice and Grandma laugh."

"Sounds like a good shot," Strep said.

"It is, but since then I've always wondered why Mom never cut Grandpa Robinson out of the picture." Fiona looked at Strep. "Grandma looks so pretty and alive, just glowing like a bride should, and I know Mom would never want to throw that away. But the justice of the peace is right between her and grandpa. It would be so easy to just snip it there and he'd be gone."

"Maybe it's the only picture she has of him."

"Probably." The same thought occurred to Fiona every time she pulled the photo out. There were no others in any of her mom's drawers, none she could find anywhere in the house. If Mom threw it out, he would be entirely gone from their lives. She could have made him disappear but had decided not to for some reason. Mom may say she was better off without him, may act all angry, but finding the photo made Fiona realize her mom held onto some kind of hope about her own father. It was easy to dismiss him with words, but her actions said there was something more going on. She was holding on to that picture for some reason. Fiona wondered if Mom ever just pulled it out and stared at it like she did.

"Do you look like him?"

Strep's question stirred her from her thoughts. "I think I do. Mom always says I'm built just like my grandma, but the picture shows that both Grandpa and Grandma were small and thin."

"That sure sounds like you."

Fiona smiled wistfully, picturing herself staring at the photo. She'd never seen either one of her grandparents. "Yeah, he was maybe an inch or two taller than her from the looks of it." The picture made it clear that she took after both grandparents, not just Grandma Rose. She could tell from the picture, even if it was black and white, that his skin browned duskily in the summer, just as hers and Mom's did. Mom's hair was jet black, like his, while Fiona's was tempered by her dad's dull red hair into an auburn that got practically dishwater blonde in the summer and then darkened in the winter.

"And . . . ?" Strep prompted.

"He smiled like I do, too." Thinking about his smile made her smile. It was her favorite thing about the picture. She loved how Grandpa's eyes gleamed mischievously as he looked past the justice of the peace and toward Grandma Rose. Fiona's smile, whether in school portraits or selfies, had a similar glimmer. She could tell from Grandpa's smile that he had refused to go to a church, and she could tell from Grandma's smile that she was happy to go wherever he wanted. Mom could pretend that Grandpa hadn't existed, but Fiona thought that the photograph showed in more ways than one how his features and personality were stamped onto their bodies and into their lives. His features—which were theirs now—marked them as Indian, but other than how they looked, Fiona was unsure what it meant. Being Indian had to mean something because she found herself thinking about it more and more often. For Fiona that was what she missed most in her mom's silence and in not knowing her grandfather.

"Do you think he smiled just before he disappeared?" Strep asked. "I mean in his dream about the security tape." He tapped the papers balanced on his knee, his finger marking the blackbird coffee story. He turned to face her, suddenly serious as he sometimes got, and looked at her with sincere concern. "I hate to put it this way, Fee, but was he a little off? I mean talking about birds and coffee and security tape is strange. And he left your mom and grandma, right? Could he have been a little, you know, mentally ill?"

Fiona laughed. Strep, who was usually unintentionally blunt, was trying to be sensitive, asking if her grandpa was mentally ill, rather than straight up declaring that he must've been whacked out or crazy. She appreciated the effort. "I don't know if he was." She chuckled ruefully now that she really thought about it. Any man who left his wife and daughter probably really did have something wrong with him. She looked at Strep. "I don't know what he was—he could be crazy, mean, or stupid for all I know—and he's been gone for years. Way longer than I've even been alive." And Mom's silence only takes him further away, Fiona thought. He left her, and she was returning the favor, abandoning him to memories she wouldn't even talk about, burying his photo under all her socks—and she wants me to do the same. She wants me to ignore him, but that doesn't seem right.

The photo showed he was part of their lives, of her life. He was there, but as an absence, not as a body or a voice. He's a mystery, she thought, that little flutter of movement at the edge of sight, and when you turn to get a good look at it, it's gone—but maybe not as gone as Mom wished. This letter said he'd been here, writing stories. He had something to say. His words were here, even if no one had any idea where he was.

Strep slipped the story about the blackbird to the bottom of the stack. "Dude's weird," he said as he scanned down the second page. "Read this. He calls it a 'Sasquatch Thought.'"

Fiona leaned in close and looked at the page on Strep's knee. The words there were inked in neat black blocks, tiny little square letters in what she thought were ridiculously straight lines, especially since the paper was unlined. They were precise in a way that told Fiona something about who her grandpa was, even if she wasn't sure what she was being told, but the words there seemed like they could be Sasquatch's.

You and them woods, men. You and them trees. Shake my head, men. Trees you see. Trees! you holler. Home I holler. Listen! Me in them woods, men. Me, your dream.

Leave them trees alone, men. Trees, twisted thickets of spruce, men. You know twisted thickets, men, your head, them woods, yet the bog at the center, the muck there, the murk there, you only dream. Skinny legs sunk in swamp, them trees. Them trees, I scratch my chin with them. Dream is what we are, the bog there, me, the murk at the center of what you holler to see, men.

Dreamstep I do, big foot ramble through spruce, through dreams, through muck. Me in the deep spruce there, see me men, yet them pictures you make, them show only swamp shadow and murk dream. Proof you call it.

Proof! you holler. You holler it again and keep hollering, yet men doubt your dream, men.

Dream men! Dream! Holler that! Proof is no proof!

Listen! Them bog foot swampstep show me. Yet, men, twisted steps sunk in muck are evidence of absence only, men, yet absence points deeper men, under the muck men, dream deeper.

"I told you it was weird," Strep said. "And that's what I mean about mentally ill, Fee. On one page he's disappearing inside a mall and on the next he thinks he's Sasquatch out in the swamp." Strep frowned, probably thinking of his own struggles at school. "I know he's writing in English, but I don't think it's the kind of English that Mr. Sjostrom would give a passing grade."

Fiona smiled. Strep had a point. It was weird, but weirder still, as she read down the page, she had begun to see Grandpa Robinson's small dark hand—the one she knew from the photograph, only more wrinkled, older—carefully writing out the words just before she read them. Carefully shaping each letter, making sure his line stayed straight.

Strep flipped to the next page. "Still weird," he flatly declared. "Still squatchy." Fiona, eager to see, grabbed the bundle from Strep and began to read.

Them trees are men, men. Listen! Them men, not dreams, men.

Trees dream men. And you men people them twisted thickets with fear, the shadow of big feet, the murk and muck of men. Men dream monsters; treemares, men—holler that! Fear tree dreams, men. That's you men, treemares. Fear men, men. Holler fear!

And yet you pour through them trees, men, water pounding over rock, you the water, and them bootfeet pound the home ground flat.

Flat with fear, men, pound it flat. Look men, no foot, no print. Holler me: Men, my home is not flat! Holler that!

Dream shadow feet among the trees, men. Find tracks under tree crowns, men, find them in roots. Measure track dreams in inches, men, measure them in plaster. Men, make yourselves in inches and plaster; men, lose yourselves in inches and plaster. Lose yourself, men; lose fear dreams, lose inches, lose plaster. Lose yourself.

Find me.

Examining the empty box while Fiona finished reading, Strep asked, "What was your grandpa's name again?"

Fiona looked up from the page. "Robinson," she said. "Robinson Heroux."

"Then who's J. E. S.?" Strep tapped the square for the return address on the box.

Fiona looked at it: J. E. S., PO Box 343, Bigfork, MN 56628.

"And where's Bigfork? Up north somewhere?" Puzzled, Strep shook his head. He looked at her. "Is that where your grandpa lives?" Strep was not fond of mysteries.

"I don't know," she said. "To be honest, I guess I always thought he was dead." She squared the papers on her knees and put the two envelopes on top of them. "Mom sure makes it seem that way."

Strep's phone brayed. "I like that donkey sound," he had explained when Fiona asked about the ringtone earlier in the summer. "It's good to be warned if some jackass is calling."

It brayed a second time.

"It's Mom," he said.

"Not a jackass, then."

"Oh, she has her moments," Strep said as he read the incoming texts.

Fiona smiled. Classic Strep.

Looking up from his phone, Strep said, "Gotta go. On the first one, Mom says the *turf* at the *abode* needs mowing." He over-enunciated the words from their eighth-grade vocabulary lessons, or ones that sounded like they might be from their vocab lessons. It was a game they'd played all summer. Fiona had started it. She thought strange words made common things sounds more interesting. Kind of like these things Grandpa writes about, she thought, glancing down at the Sasquatch words balanced on her knee.

"On the second one, she says, 'Lots of love, Mr. Strepkowski.'" Smiling, Strep leapt from the top step to the sidewalk and started toward home. "See you at Dane's later?" he asked. "His parents are checking Chance out of the hospital as we speak, but I bet he's still seeing visions and hearing the voices tell him all those strange thoughts." Chance, Dane's older brother, had been hospitalized time and again over the last year. Schizophrenia. "You know I love to hear those trippy things he says."

"I'll be there," she said, watching him walk down the block.

Going over to Dane's was one of the rituals of summer. The three of them—and Chance, when he was out of the hospital—spent almost every night hanging out at the picnic table in Dane's backyard, playing cards and talking. They didn't just talk about school and the tools who strived so hard to impress their teachers—she, Strep, and Dane found nothing so *contemptible* (another vocab word) as the tools who so transparently brownnosed for good grades, but they had also spent a lot of time in recent weeks talking about their ideas about the world and religion and life. She couldn't help but regard them as quite mature conversations. Things that needed to be thought about.

Strep spun around and shouted back to her from halfway down the block. "You can tell us about your grandpa then. I bet he wasn't crazy at all. I bet he was a spy, or in the witness protection program, or something. Something where he had to keep a low profile. That's why nobody knows anything about him. I bet those letters explain it all, Fee. Everything." He spun back around and continued on his way.

Fiona tucked the papers and the envelopes under her arm and grabbed the box. "Who is J. E. S.?" she said as she looked at the shaky initials scrawled there. They were not as neat and precise as her grandpa's writing. She also noticed that the box was addressed to "Fiona Heroux MacGowan." That was a detail she hadn't caught when they had come up the walk toward her house. As soon as Strep had seen the box leaning against the front door, he had bound up the steps and grabbed it before she could.

"My middle name is Rose," she told the box, not expecting it would understand, but saying it anyway. "Heroux was Grandpa and Grandma's last name, the one Mom was born with." One of the only things Mom had told her about her grandpa was that Heroux was a French name and that lots of Indians in northern Minnesota had French last names. "For a couple hundred years, the French and the Indians traded and sometimes those Indian women took a French husband,"

Mom had explained. "But because of the way that man treated Grandma Rose, I was happy to change it to MacGowan when your father and I got married." As she stood staring at the box, and thinking about how her mom spoke, Fiona suddenly realized that Mom never referred to Grandpa Robinson as her father. He was always *that man* or *him*. She regarded him as contemptuously as Fiona did the brownnosers at school.

"He left when Grandma Rose got sick the first time," was all Mom would offer when Fiona asked for more stories about him. "I was younger than you then, but I nursed Grandma through that first cancer and we took care of one another until the second one got her when I was at college, long before I met your dad and had you."

Mom loved her mother, and stories about Grandma Rose abounded. Pictures of her hung on the walls or leaned in frames on the mantel and note cards containing Grandma's special recipes were tucked in between the pages of the cookbooks on the kitchen shelf. While she loved the grandma she had never met, all questions about her were answered. She was alive in Fiona's imagination because of the pictures Mom painted, but this Grandpa, rarely spoken of, this hole in her life, had captured her for some reason. The mystery of him, their Indianness. "He's a cipher," Fiona said aloud, exercising another of those vocab words.

As she looked at the box, and thought about her mom's feelings, Fiona knew it would be best if her parents didn't know about what J. E. S. had sent her until later—if ever. If he had wanted them to know, he wouldn't have addressed the package to her.

She unlocked the front door and went up to her room. Closing the door, she ditched the box under her bed and promised herself: "I'll find a better hiding place for it later." She jumped up on the bed, crossed her legs in front of her, and set the sheaf of papers, the opened letter, and the unopened envelope addressed "To: the Grandchild" on the comforter in front of her. Grandpa's stories called strongly to her, but that letter addressed to "Fiona" was open. It had said these stories were from her grandpa. She picked it up and began to read. Maybe it would help make sense of these stories her grandpa had sent her. If the rest were anything like the first few had been, she'd need some help.

PART TWO

Letters and Stories

Dear Fiona,

You don't know me, but I knew your grandfather at the end of his life. He asked me to send you the stories he'd written. He told me stories are meant to help people, but I'm not sure what kind of help you will find in his words.

He died four years before you were born—or at least social media shows your birthday being four years later. I think he died then, but I don't really know—let's just say the last time I saw him was four years before you were born. He didn't know you were you, that you were a girl named Fiona. He said your middle name would be Heroux, so I addressed it that way to you. Fiona Heroux MacGowan. He said *heroux* meant happy in French, but he was wrong. That's *heureux*, so I don't know why he said that.

He didn't know if you were going to be a boy or a girl—he hadn't seen you in a dream or anything. He just knew one day your mom would have a baby. He always referred to you as "*the* grandchild," not "the grandchild" as in "the ball," but *the* grandchild. *That* one, *the* one. He talked about you every day he stayed with me, how you'd need him one day, how he'd help you understand something about being a lost little Indian child. *Anishinaabe*, not *Indian*—I can hear him correct me even after he's been gone all these years. An Anishinaabe child with little sense of what it means to be Anishinaabe. He described himself as also lost, but said he wrote stories that helped him make sense of loss, or that wrestled with loss, or that seemed to suggest he found some sort of answers in making up these stories—or something like that. I'm not sure. I've enclosed them in this box for you. You can decide for yourself.

He told me to send you the stories in eighteen years. He said there is an ancient earthwork mound in Ohio, or someplace—maybe Idaho—he told me a lot in those couple days he spent with me, so I might get some things confused. I remember the important part of what he said, though. Every eighteen years the moon rises over a particular part of this earthwork. He said it was a generational clock. "You can set your watch and your family by it," he told me. Eighteen years was a generational marker. He said it was the amount of time a baby takes to develop into a young adult, and he also said it was the amount of time it takes for a newly departed person to develop spiritual maturity. He said to send you his writing when his departed spirit was eighteen years old. I don't know where he got some of these ideas. Some I think were his alone, sourceless, but I promised to send you this package in eighteen years, so here you go.

I've read all the stories in here, a time or two at least. I read the ones about the outer space Indians at least once a year for some reason—well, I must admit I'm a bit of a sci-fi buff, but I've never read what's in the envelope addressed to *the* grandchild. He said that was for you alone. The stories puzzle me, because I think he's often telling them about himself, while at other times I suppose he's writing about people he met, but he only refers to himself as "I" once, in the story about the blackbird. Sometimes he writes about himself as Robinson, sometimes just as "he." In one story he writes from his father's point of view. Sometimes he talks about historical battles and events, but I don't think what he says is ever a fact. Imagine a fat priest in a canoe three hundred years ago doubting his calling. I sometimes don't know what he was thinking, your old granddad, but I'd definitely avoid using his stories in any reports to your history class! Ha-ha.

He uses "I" in a few other of these writings of his, but it's Bigfoot speaking in them, not your grandfather. I don't really understand why. He said he'd been expecting to see a Sasquatch for years, *dying* to see one he said, and I ruined it when I rescued him and dragged him back to my shack up here near Bigfork. See, he'd wounded a deer—out of season as it turns out, your grandfather was that kind of guy, I guess. He tracked it from morning until late in the January afternoon. "Couldn't let the animal bleed out. Got to respect it, Jimmy, got to respect the old ways and what they teach about the deer people. Got to give it the mercy shot and end its misery," is what he told me.

Fiona paused on that line. One mystery sort of solved. J.E.S. was someone named Jimmy.

I didn't know what he meant by the deer people, I just took it to be an Indian thing. "Anishinaabe!" Yes, I still hear him correcting me every day. Maybe when his spirit matures his voice will leave me alone. But I was telling you about rescuing him.

So he tracked that deer all day long and even before night fell, even before twilight, his legs gave out. He was an old man at that point in his life. He was too weak to walk. "That's how much I loved that deer, Jimmy," he told me. "I walked until I was ready to die, just like I knew he would do. I couldn't deliver the mercy shot, but the deer people would see I was trying."

The snow wasn't very deep that year, but he piled fallen leaves and what snow he could reach over his legs, hoping they would hold his body heat in. He ate the last little bit of a candy bar he had in his pocket and then leaned back against the tree where he had settled. "I thought the deer might come stumbling by," he told me later. "I could kill it and use his body as a blanket, kind of like Custer did with that horse." At the time I thought he was delusional, but then I found the answer to that little bit of talk in one of the stories enclosed with this letter. I won't say anymore. You'll find out soon enough.

Your grandpa continued with his story, telling me, "But as night fell I knew no deer would come stumbling by. There was little hope of that, and that's when I began to sing," he told me. "When hope ran out."

It was a death song, he said. I realized later that it was just like the song the Indians in space hear coming out of a black hole.

This all comes later, of course. Right now, you're wondering how he ended up at my shack, so I'll tell you.

I often go out and hike in the woods at night. In the winter, even on a moonless night, the snow makes the woods as bright as a city street and as quiet as a painting. Just shadows and light, Fiona, just the tools all artists use. You should try it sometime.

There was a quarter moon that night, the full moon having passed, and when you walk in the woods, all bundled against the cold—and I'm sure it was below zero that night—all you hear is your own breath and the crunch of your boots on the dry snow. Then I heard this chuffing sound. You don't usually see deer on a freezing night, but the sound was like those little snorting sounds a deer does. *Chuff, chuff.* I peered into the trees off the path. *Chuff.* I pulled my hat off and leaned toward the sound and then heard it more plainly. *Chuff, chuff-uff, chuff chuff chuff.* There was enough rhythm there that I knew I wasn't listening to a deer. I called, "Who's out there?" There was no answer but I could still hear the rhythm so I ran toward it, pausing to stop and listen and reset my bearings every few yards. "Hello! Anyone there!" I kept calling. "Sing out if you can hear me." But he never said a word, just kept chuffing that song. Singing out I guess, but I don't think he was responding to my call.

I emerged into a little clearing and found him leaning against that tree, still just singing, his head nodding down towards his chest. He looked three-quarters dead. As I rushed across the clearing I yelled, "Hey, man, you must be freezing out here." He stopped in midsong and looked up at me lumbering in all my winter gear towards him. "*Boozhoo Mi-sah-bay!*" His voice was stronger in words than in song. "I've been waiting for you."

I learned later that *boozhoo* is how Anishinaabe say hello. He told me how to spell it. I never found out what *mi-sah-bay* meant, but I've always assumed it was the Indian word for friend or rescuer or something.

"I'm Jimmy," I told him.

"I'm lost," he said. "I knew you'd come. *Mi-sah-bay*"—his voice hesitated on each syllable—"takes care of Anishinaabe."

I didn't know what he was talking about, so I just told him my name again and began to strip off my coat and dig through the layers of leaves and snow on his legs. His pants were soaked through. I tried to stand him up, tried to wrap my coat around his shoulders, but he just slid back down to the ground. "Let me sit," he mumbled.

"We've got to get you warmed up." I wrapped my coat around his legs. I knew the only way to get him out of there was to get the toboggan and drag him home. "You remember that song, old man? What you were singing a minute ago?"

He nodded. "It's the song my dad tried to sing when he was dying," he said and began to mutter the words again. I could tell his lungs were filled with something; could tell it was hard for him to breathe.

"Just keep singing until I get back, okay?" I sprinted back to my shack then, grabbed a couple of wool army surplus blankets, and stoked up the fire in the woodstove. I grabbed the old toboggan I used to drag firewood to the cabin and ran back to your grandpa. He was still singing. Weakly.

His eyes were glassy and he looked up at me as I settled him in the blankets on the toboggan. "*Mi-sah-bay*," he said again. "Take me with you. Let me live where you live."

"I'm taking you back to my shack," I told him. "It's warm there."

I got him back to the cabin, laid him on the floor next to the roaring stove, got him out of those soaking clothes and rolled him up in blankets. "You get some sleep, old fella. You'll be warm now." He mumbled something more about *mi-sah-bay* and warmth in the night. Said it was what love felt like, dark and warm. When he warmed up a bit, I lifted his slight body—he was a small man, Fiona, he could've hid behind a birch tree if he wanted—and moved him onto my old couch and pushed it closer to the stove. He later told me you'd be like he was—slightly built, birdlike, light-boned—and it would bug the hell out of your mom to see that little bit of him in her house every day.

"He's right," Fiona said. "It drives her crazy sometimes." At other times, though, she'd catch her mom looking wistfully at her as she ran up to the house or dashed out back to chase the neighbor's dog out of their flower garden. There must have been moments when Mom wondered what had become of Grandpa Robinson, Fiona thought as she continued to read.

His lips were blue when I went to bed but they flared bright red overnight. He went from nearly frozen to death to burning with fever in the space of a few hours.

"Let's get you to the hospital, friend."

"Robinson," he croaked his name, then took a sip of the tea I'd given him. "You're only my friend if you let me be. No hospital."

So I let him be and over the next two days he told me everything I'd need to know, as he put it. He told me about the grandchild. He told me he was squatting at some weekender's cabin over on Clear Lake off County Road 31. Most weekenders weren't ice fishermen, so they never came up in the winter. "I broke in," he told me, "but I keep it clean. They won't even know I've been there when spring comes." He chuffed, smiling grimly. "Won't know, except for the broken window." He looked at me, his eyes still glazed. "I fixed it with a piece of cardboard."

He proceeded to tell me he'd spent the last five winters squatting in different cabins, poaching game, feeding himself, and writing pages and pages of his thoughts that he then whittled down into stories for *the* grandchild. He never said what he did during the summer, never said what he did before five years ago. He coughed a lot, telling me these stories. Racking, hacking coughs that felt like they wanted to bring something out of his chest, but couldn't. He said he was disappointed that I had no instant coffee, but he drank cup after cup of the tea I offered him. He wouldn't eat anything; he claimed he had no appetite anymore. It was clear that whatever was in his lungs—what I wanted to take him to the hospital for—was getting worse.

"I won't be here much longer," he told me on the third morning. "Tell me you'll get the stories for me and bring them back here. You'll find my stories just sitting on the dining table." He coughed. "I put a big rock on top of the pages so they wouldn't blow around if the cardboard popped out of the window." He looked at me. "There's an envelope, too, with a letter for the grandchild." A wave of coughing seized him for a minute. When it cleared, he rasped weakly, "Don't forget the letter. I wrote it last summer."

I knew he needed to get to the hospital and thought if he had the stories it'd be easier to get him to go. "I can get them today if you want."

He nodded a thanks and in between coughs he stared blankly at the guitars in the corner. Your grandpa never asked what I was doing out in the woods in a shack, never asked about my guitars and the little recording studio I'd rigged up in the corner of the room. It had been my great-uncle's house, but after he died the family had kept it for a hunting shack. I'd retreated there after my girlfriend dumped me. I was going to record away my grief in songs, living the winter out in music and sorrow and art, all to make an album that would touch the heart-wounded everywhere. I ended up never completing a song and never leaving the cabin. I still live here. Since then I've made my money as a web designer, just living out in the woods, working freelance.

"That would be good if you could get them today," he told me. "I left the door unlocked." He told me about the earthworks then and asked me to send the stories to you, the grandchild, if he was unable to. "Tidy the place up, too, would you?" It was an easy promise to make and that evening when I got back from my little foray to the cabin at Clear Lake, he was gone. The couch was pushed back into place and the blankets were neatly folded and put on the shelf where I usually kept them. If I hadn't had his stories in my hand, I might have doubted he'd ever been there.

Realizing he was gone—and fearing the fever had made him crazy, I ran out into the yard and tracked his boot prints in the thin snow. They led into the deep part of the woods, into a thick swamp, but night had fallen by then. I listened for that singing chuff, that song he'd weakly sang, but heard nothing. I called his name. I called *boozhoo*. I called *mi-sah-bay*, but got nothing. His tracks disappeared in a damp part of the swamp. There must have been a spring under the mud there, bubbling up from deep in the warm part of the earth, because the muck and wetness of it was not frozen. His tracks ended there. I could see nothing. The dark swamp water was not like the bright snow on the paths in the woods. It absorbed light the way it absorbed your grandfather's steps.

I went back to the cabin and reported his disappearance to the sheriff and the next morning a halfhearted crew of deputies and volunteers undertook a search in the convenient parts of the woods and dragged a hook through the swamp, then called off the search after less than two days. "His body will surface after the thaw," the deputy in charge told me.

After they gave up, I continued to search for him for two more days, covering miles, peering in the windows of the weekenders' cabins on the other side of the swamp, down on Radisson Lake, and saw no sign of him. I skirted the swamp, looking for where his boots might have left tracks when he exited it and found nothing. Four days had then passed and I reasoned he was either dead or had somehow evaded all search—but he'd been too sick for that. I hadn't wanted to believe it, and I hate to share it with you, but the only place he could have gone was into that dark swamp water. I wish I could say he pulled open a door in the thick air above the swamp and stepped into a warm, light place. Hope makes you dream such thoughts.

Off and on over the next few weeks I picked through the frozen parts of the swamp looking for his body during the day and working on my music at night, though I often found myself reading his words instead of recording. I tried adapting some of the stories into songs, with no luck, but found that the challenge distracted me from thoughts of my ex. I found my idea to sing heart-wrecked songs to lonely people sort of cold and lonely itself. No one wants to take a sad walk to that kind of dark swamp. After a few weeks, I put his stories under the folded blankets on the shelf so he could keep them warm. I took them out occasionally, to dip here and there in them, but mostly I let them rest up for their trip to you. Then I waited the requested eighteen years, though technically I guess it's really only seventeen and a half since he wandered off on a cold January night and I'm sending them to you on a humid July morning. I think since he wrote the letter to you the summer before he disappeared, the stories should arrive eighteen years from that time, not eighteen years after his death. His letter for you must be like that death song he was singing.

Even after seventeen and a half years his body has never surfaced, so maybe he did pass through some door that none of the rest of us could see. Maybe he broke a pane out of the window of that door and got into a place he was never meant to be. If he did, I'm sure he mended the break with a piece of celestial cardboard. I guess I'm saying, maybe he was there all along, floating above the swamp and over each of us during that ragged search Deputy Kamminga led. I never thought to look up. Hope, again, leads me to think he might have been watching us.

Dream thoughts won't get you anywhere, Fiona.

Still, I hope Robinson was wrong. I hope you're not a little lost child and I hope his stories make you happy—*heureux* or Heroux—if that's what you want. That's what he wanted I think. I'm not sure there's really too much useful information about your family in these stories, but I guess they'll give you a sense of what sorts of things gave him pause to wonder and what sort gave him pause to worry. I'm sure they reveal something about who he was, but whatever those things are I'm pretty sure they're not the kind of things you'd read in an obituary. Like I said, his stories are not very fact oriented. I hope you enjoy them for what they are.

My best to you,

Jimmy

Fiona let the final page of the letter drop down on top of the others. Jimmy was able to answer a lot of her questions; he'd told her lots of things she'd never have otherwise known. Lots of stuff her mom probably didn't even know. Grandpa sang death songs, he poached and broke into people's cabins, and he disappeared on a cold night—so completely that even a search party couldn't find him. She shook her head thinking about some of these things he did. Breaking into cabins and poaching were illegal, and walking into a swamp in the middle of winter seemed suicidal for an old man, yet there was something to be admired there as well, she thought. Even if what he did was illegal, no one got hurt from his actions. "Well, I guess the deer did," she had to admit, but still found herself pleased to realize that he seemed to have his own mind and he knew how to take care of himself, even if it was in a way that most people would disapprove of.

She grabbed her phone off the nightstand and located Bigfork with the mapping app. It was up north, like Strep had guessed, and with a few more minutes searching she found Clear Lake, where Grandpa had squatted, and Radisson Lake where Jimmy had searched for him. Switching to Earth view gave her a sense of where the area was forested and where the swamps might be, even the one by Radisson Lake. She stared at it and thought, That's his last resting place. It was so tiny on her screen, so small that she zoomed in on it. The closer she pulled it in, the more the image fragmented into little squares that revealed nothing at all. The little, pixelated squares of the fully zoomed-in map reminded her of the squared-off letters her grandpa had precisely scribed on sheets of unlined paper.

She set the letter down, but before she picked up the sheaf of stories, she looked again at her phone. She zoomed out until the image resolved back into something that looked like a swamp. I'll just have to go there, she thought. See what it really looks like. Maybe I will find something of his there, or maybe I can leave something of mine for him.

She picked up the stories, turned past the one about the blackbird and the two Sasquatch rants—at least that's how they struck her, eager to see what her grandpa had to say. Glancing at her phone, she could see she had at least two or three hours before either Mom or Dad would get home from work.

Swampbreath

Listen, men! I holler what men know. I holler what men walk away from. Listen!

Swamp shuddered, men, swamp exhaled. A dank mist swelled from swamp lung into earth air, men. A body stood there, the swamp's breath, a dark form near the trees, and I strode toward it, men, and I entered it. Me, fully formed in four long steps. I burst from the murk there, men, from mist into body, from breath into life. Like that, men, easy. Me! I holler. I did not search, men, I found.

Men, you seek form. Holler that! Men did not walk into men form, as I walked into mine. You walked toward it, men, millions of dank steps. Walked out of water into muck onto land and up into the trees, men, up into the green clouds of tree crowns! You men were men then—ape, for true.

Up there in the leaf rain, men, you rose toward the sun. Holler that! Bare teeth and bounce on tree branch, men, make the green cloud tremble. Holler, tumble, swing, men—be men, men; be ape. Keep to the green cloud, men, and swing through them trees, but don't slip; keep to the branches, men, but don't fall. Holler to the sky, men, swing toward the light, branch up, men, and up again. Your form found.

Yet slip men did; yet fall you fell, men. Drawn from trembling tree crowns to hard ground. Branch bouncing left no footprints and you men want evidence of your own importance. Footprints, you holler! See there, you holler! There, you stub-finger point: A footprint! Me, you holler, my form found!

Out of the green rain you jumped to earth, men; from out of the sky and onto the homeground you jump, men; and you leave them footprints to measure your importance. You leave midden pile monuments to your form, men, piles of rocks and bones and the shit of what you ate, men, as evidence of your importance: Your footprints.

Where you find them footprints, men, you dig holes and then, men, you fill them holes with houses. You build yourself back inside trees, men, houses made from dead branches. I see trees, you see houses. Still the ape, men, yet now hidden from light and the green rain. I live, you holler! Look at that hole, you holler, that house is my footprint!

But I see what men walk away from, men.

I see houses become cities, men, and cities become nations. I see nations become wars, men. Don't walk away from that, men! Let me holler now. Listen!

War is a towering dead tree, men, the form of your footprint, evidence of your importance. You make war and you make graves, men: you make monuments to the footprints of the dead.

I shake my head, men. Listen. I want to cry. Your footprints are empty graves, men, waiting to be filled; monuments to the true form of men, war.

Men, I holler! Men, I bare my teeth.

Listen! Spring back to the greencloud of the tree crown, men, spring back into the green rain! Walk away from the form you found, men.

Walk away, men. Your footprints are dead nations.

The Horse Chrysalis

Custer saw all his possible deaths converging. Every one of them coming his way. Arrows, volleys of bullets, war clubs. Indians swarming below the ridge. Cavalry sabers wrested from the already dead used on the soon to be. Knives, hatchets. Sioux, Cheyenne. Gunshot—American, Indian—snapped the air. He thought of God, his Father. He thought of home.

He saw his scalp on the poles outside the Indian camps. Saw his teeth stove in, falling to the back of his throat, and he coughed. He saw his eyeballs fingered from their sockets, their fluid drained by the Indians the way pretty girls drain juice from quartered oranges.

Custer watched his men fall and become strange prairie creatures prickled with arrowshafts. Watched them fleeing, then falling. No escape, even with prayers on their lips.

He saw his scrotum hacked from his loins, the sac fashioned into one of the Sioux pouches, full of their tobacco. Saw his testicles flung into the scrubby brush on the hillside, food for the gophers.

He listened to his men crying, invoking God's help, blaspheming their Father's name, calling out for loved ones—for mothers, wives, and lovers as yet unmet and unmarried. He thought of his Elizabeth, their never-conceived children simmering in the stomachs of gophers. He thought of home.

The battle was a drumbeat. Indian voices raised in song as American blood seeped into native soil.

A horse toppled on a nearby slope, breath rasping in its throat. He thought of his Elizabeth. The horse laboring in its last moments.

He saw his death in the horse's death, and then he saw his only choice. He saw his home in the horse. He slit the horse's belly as it kicked against the pain and pulled its guts from the cavity. Intestines, stomach, heart, liver pushed against his knees, their warmth competing against the pounding sun overhead. He pulled the uterus from the horse's gut and a tiny fetus stared up at him, shiny white through the membrane, eyes as flat and black as jacket buttons. An albino. He slit its throat and crawled inside the horse. A small act of mercy. He drew the flaps of horseskin together and held them closed with bloodied hands. He rocked inside the horse and its body slipped and slid down the slope, away from the pile of guts, fooling the Sioux.

He thought of home.

The lady from the church had given Yellow Bird the little diary a month ago. "Record your prayers here, let our Father know your wishes." It fit in the pocket of the dungarees all the boys wore.

She didn't call him Yellow Bird though. She called him Joseph. White names had been written on a blackboard when he arrived at the school three years ago. One by one the children were handed a long stick and instructed to touch the name they wanted. Being American was being free to choose, he later learned. Once a name was selected, Teacher erased the name from the board and recorded it in a book. Joseph. He had liked the curl of the *J* chalked on the board. It reminded him of the way his mother's hair curved on her back when pulled into a ponytail. Her dark hair, a gentle wave so black in the sunlight it seemed almost blue. His dark hair was streaked with yellow strands, the mark of his perhaps father. Inverted, the *J* was a kind of question mark. The curve of his mother's ponytail flipped upside down in his memory.

Yellow Bird thought about his mother every day. Me-o-tzi. *Spring Grass* in this white language. Her father—his grandfather—killed in battle by Long Hair, the white soldier Custer, at the Washita River encampment eight years before Custer met his own death at the Little Big Horn—five years ago now. He thought everyday about his father. His mother became the killer's lover according to the old crows who unlike his grandfather lived to gossip about the battle and its survivors. She lay down with him and months later the child with yellow strands woven through the black cried its first questions. The milk of her breasts the first answer. Love, of course. A mother always giving, but never any answers after that. Only the gossip of crows. Their withered breasts were bitter grass to his memory.

Air inside the horse was thick, dense with the damp stench of slaughter. Custer's long hair was dank with raw blood. Death smelled like warm blood cooling. It was dark in there, black, but it felt red; a red midnight—a dying fire and black stars. His face pressed against the slick flesh of the horse's ribs, he could taste what was left of its life cooling against his lips. He tasted spring grass on his tongue and it filled his mouth like a memory. Like something he once knew. Like home, like Elizabeth, but not home, not Elizabeth. He pulled the flaps of horseskin closer together, hiding himself against the memory, and the body of the horse tightened around him. When he breathed, the horse breathed with him. The Sioux would see the movement if there was any. He felt its body move as he filled his lungs. He thought about the Indians and held his breath.

Sound inside the horse was muffled. The drum of his heart beat in his ears. Feet rushed past for a while, whoops and shouts penetrated the horse's body as distant noises, and the snap of bullets became dull thumps.

Then—

Crack!

And again—

Crack!

Not dull thumps.

The horse's body jerked with the shots and Custer felt lead graze his temple and then the flash of a bullet burst in his chest. The horse was not armor. The horse was flesh and he began to bleed into it, his life spilling into its belly.

He thought of home and weakened, his grasp on his body slipped and he drew heaving breaths. Helpless, he began to push against the pain, his boots kicking at the horse's pelvis. He thought of his Father; he thought of home. His Elizabeth. He kicked but his kick was only a weak push anymore. He thought of tender grass on the prairie below him.

He hadn't seen this death coming. Hadn't seen his body opening like a book, folding back until its covers touched and the pages fanned out, every one of them exposed. Hadn't seen his heart becoming the horse's heart, his intestines becoming the horse's guts, his testicles becoming the horse's ovaries. Hadn't seen his body folding back into itself, a spent shell.

Joseph. The lady from the church said it was the name of her Lord's father. Not his father, really, but the man he called father. Her Lord was like Yellow Bird. He knew a man and he knew many stories, but he never really knew his father. He had never held his hand or learned to track from him, had never learned the ways of horses or men from him, and really only ever had his dreams of the man that some said was his father.

"Comanche!"

The sound outside was sharp, no longer dull. Custer's eyes jerked open. It was light, day.

"It's not."

He felt a shiver run through his flesh, a rippling quiver that rose from the loins into the spine and up into the base of his skull. He rocked where he lay, his eye fixed on a cloud above. It was alone. White in the blue, then he rose to four feet. He felt a weight slip from his belly. He stumbled down the hill toward the two talking men.

"It is."

"Look here."

One man put a hand on his flank.

"What do you see?"

He turned his head and saw the two soldiers squatting there, examining his loins.

"Nothing."

"Comanche's a stallion."

He knew Comanche as Captain Keogh's mount.

"Whose mare is this, then?"

The soldiers were filthy, the kind of men sent in to collect the dead after battle—to bundle them up and pack them on wagons for the journey home. They were smoking, these soldiers, gray tendrils trickling from their noses and lips. Tobacco smoke against the stench of death he now realized filled his own head. Days must have passed since battle. One of the soldiers smacked his rump and he stumbled back up the slope.

"That old pack horse has seen better days," one of the men said.

Pack horse. He turned at the lip of the ridge and looked at the scattered dead, the strange transformations of battle. The three-eyed man prone at his feet, two eyes brown, one red, darkening to black around the edges on his left cheek. The man with the exposed brain, the shell of his skull placed like a dish on his chest; the man with arms but no hands; the man with a rusted knife where his tongue once was. The man who was twenty feet long—who had dragged himself to die in the shade of a bush, his path marked by a strew of blood and intestine.

"He's here!"

He turned to the shout and saw a soldier down the slope standing over a body. Heard the soldier yell, "It's Custer!"

His horse brain couldn't make sense of the words. Words were impressions, feelings, like a pat on the neck, more than information. He felt a rope loop around his neck and a hand stroking his withers.

"There you go, old girl."

He turned to the voice. Another soldier, this one with a handful of horses leashed to ropes behind him.

"There you go," he patted again and knotted the rope. "We'll get you home." The soldier held some sugar cubes under his mouth. He took them in without thought.

He followed the soldier and the other horses the rest of the day until finally he was hobbled and set out to graze well away from the battlefield. The grass was trampled flat where it wasn't torn, but he was able to fill his belly. He thought of Elizabeth and she tasted like grass.

The next days were measured in steps and effort. His leg tore on a sharp stone and the wound festered until it became a limp. Still, he sometimes pulled a laden wagon as one day rounded into the next. Sometimes he walked behind it, drawn forward by a rope tied to its back gate.

The stink of the dead hung over the wagon in a thick cloud of flies. They buzzed his eyes and lit in his wound. Maggots began to churn there. Soldiers, always smoking, sifted lime over the dead to stifle the smell. These dead began to wither as the lime leached the moisture from their bodies and pulled their flesh so taut that sharp edges of bone began to pierce through the skin. Every man a frozen grimace. He saw all this, but knew nothing of it. Grass was everything, was Elizabeth. Water in the creeks and lakes was everything else, his father. Home was this long walk.

But home became a train yard. Men herded into long cars, the dead relegated to those at the rear of the train. Horses reared and bolted but were forced eventually into still other cars. The wounded were culled from the herd and tied to a fence.

The soldier with the ropes pressed sugar cubes under his nose. "That leg's just no good." The soldier rubbed his neck, long soothing strokes that became tender stalks of grass in his horse thoughts. "I'm afraid it's the glue factory for you, old girl." The soldier's hand fell from his shoulder and sweetness melted on his tongue. He lowered his head and found a tuft of grass growing next to the fencepost. He ate. Elizabeth. Sweet grass. Home.

Yellow Bird had filled the diary, had run out of pages and so was now filling the endpapers with his words. The glue binding the endpapers to the rigid covers softened under the paper when his hand warmed it and the endpapers were now pocked with little bubbles of air that dimpled where the nib of his pen pressed on them and the ink there bled into the paper and the glue. His words becoming ink becoming glue. Teacher had told him the glue binding books like the diary was made from dead horses—their bones, tendons, and hooves boiled into this something else and made useful even in death. The lady from the church said her Father did the same to man's living soul. Made it something else in death. His words were dead horses, were living souls. The ink ran under his hand, the nib of the pen digging into the last white corner of the endpaper. His words tore the paper and the warmed glue seeped out from the tear and covered the tip of his pen.

Yellow Bird touched the nib to his tongue—the bitter gall of the ink tanged there a moment and then became something else. The taste of spring grass filled his mouth, sugar melted on his tongue, and the cool water of warm days rippled down his throat. He thought of his mother. Of home. The father he never knew.

He squeezed more glue from the tear, dabbed his fingertip in it, and brought it to his nose. He smelled the musk of a horse and saw his grandfather's mount, saw the lather of it after a long day's ride. It filled his head with home again, and then it shifted. He saw its gut pulsing and churning, as if filled with something unnatural, something other than horse, and he watched it split open and a cascade of maggots spill from the belly and cover the ground in a seething white mass. He thought of death then, of the father he never knew. He smelled the blood and the buzzing flies and threw the diary into the fire that warmed the boys' dormitory if you got close enough to it. The diary fell open, the covers folding back until they touched one another, and Yellow Bird saw the glue bubbling and dripping out onto the hot coals. Dead horses in the embers. The pages of the diary fanned open and he saw the words he had written there, his prayers, the same few words filling every page—me home Father bring me home Father bring me—laid end to end in a chain of hope that reached for that something he never knew but that now turned to flame, to ash, to smoke, and vanished up the pipe of the chimney.

Fiona looked up from the page, but the image of the diary dripping glue into the fire stuck with her. Her grandpa certainly painted strong pictures with words, things she could see as clearly as if they were in front of her. Still, the story disappointed her, as did the Sasquatch rant. Sure, they were good enough, if you liked weird nightmare sorts of things, but they really didn't tell her anything about him. They told her about men and war, about horses and what happened after that battle; they told her about that lonely boy living so far away from his mother and that Bigfoot living so far away from men, but there was nothing about Grandpa in them. Nothing. Even though Jimmy had told her not to expect much from the stories, she had hoped something would be there, some little half-hidden suggestion about her grandma or mom, some notion of what Grandpa did after he left them—or why he left. That was the big question. Instead she got an angry Sasquatch saddened by what men did, and she got some old soldier turned into a horse and a boy who never knew his father. Fantasies, it seemed. Not much to go on.

As she thought about what she wanted and what was missing in these stories, Fiona's mind began to wander. The pages in front of her blurred into a smear of words. She had something Mom didn't. Even if the stories didn't give her anything, she still had them. She smiled. They were something of his. Something better than a simple photograph. Something that was full of his thoughts, even if they weren't about what she wanted to know. They were hers now. He shared them with her, even if from beyond the grave. "Strep'll love that." Her smile widened into a grin as she imagined her friend wailing like a mournful ghost when she told him about her grandpa speaking to her from the other side.

But what about Mom? she wondered. Her smile dropped. What would Mom think? First I'd have to share them, Fiona thought, but I don't know if I can do that. Too risky. "If I were her I'd be happy, or at least curious, to see what kinds of things my dad wrote about," Fiona said, glancing at the closed door. If Mom came through it right now, if she somehow knew what Fiona was reading, she would way more likely be angry than curious. She expected that Mom would most likely just snap, grab the stories from her, and burn them or shred them or hide them, like she'd hidden that photograph. "That's not happening," Fiona muttered as she swiped the camera on her phone open. She took a quick set of photos of the pages she'd read so far, careful to center each one and make sure it was exposed properly. "What a waste," she mumbled, thinking about what she'd lose if the photos were no good. Too much light and his words would be unreadable, too dark and they'd disappear.

Holding the pages, she could almost feel the warmth of his hand as it shaped each word. She wouldn't be able to feel the photos in the same way, but she knew she needed to have a backup in case Mom angrily did something stupid with the stories. My stories, she thought, taking a picture of the last page she'd read and thinking about that lonely boy burning his own thoughts. They're mine now, even if Mom takes them away. I'll always have these, she thought as she set the phone on the bed. She smiled again. Besides, having them on her phone also meant she could read the stories at night without having to turn on a light. The light might lead Mom to her room if she left it on too late.

Warm Gravity

Men, you holler: The sun is warm! Warm in the sky above the clouds, you holler!

Reach for what's warm there, men, stretch for the sun every day, reach for it, but still them stub arms can never stretch far enough. The sun is a near star, men, but still it is far. Tremble, men. Tremble! I holler. The sun is a distant warmth.

But see, men, other warm things are near, I holler, always near! Think, men!

The sun! you holler, as if it alone is warm, men. You holler, men. You holler, The sun!

But the sun warms the air, men. Feel that. And it warms the rivers, too. Reach for that water! It warms the blood pulsing through our bodies, men. That's warm, men. The air, the river, the blood. Us, men; me, you. Listen! The sun alone is not warm.

What else is warm, men?

The sun! you holler.

What else? The air? The river?

The sun! Your stub arms reach up. You holler, dumbed by the sound of your own tongues.

Think! I bare my teeth, men, and I shake them trees. Leaves tremble down from the sky, men, in a warm green rain. Men, I holler. Think!

Listen!

Mosquitoes in the green rain are warm, men, and midges, men, and ticks. Gnats are warm too, men. All warm with the blood that pulses in trembling rivers through your stub arms and warms the muck of the swamp in your big heads. Holler that!

Now, can you feel what's warm, men?

Your dumb tongues holler, The sun! Your dumb arms rise.

The sun is warm but still, men, the earth is warm. The earth is in reach. Kneel to it men, put dumb hands on it and let what's warm there enter you. The warm earth tugs at you men, feel its pull. What pulls you, men, is gravity. Gravity is warm, men, and it pulls you down to the earth. The earth is warm gravity.

The sun's warmth can't pull you from the long dark of dumb death, men, no matter how long your reach. The earth is warm gravity, men, it tugs at you always, and pulls you on that last day into the dark grave of warm earth. That grave earth, men, is as warm as you will ever reach.

Indians in Space, Episode One: No Horizon

The door of the craft irised open and Wayne and Amos drifted out into the black well of space, tethered by long buckskin thongs to a hook on the side of the ship. Buckskin. Wayne had insisted on it.

"Ah, sweet mystery." Wayne's arm swept the vast darkness. Earth was a dim blue dot a billion miles away. "We've come a long way in a short time." He smiled behind the helmet's visor.

"Historic moment," Amos observed. "The first two Indians in space. You should say something profound, like Neil Armstrong did on the moon. 'That's one small step for man . . .'"

"I don't know," Wayne said. "I didn't prepare anything."

"We're Indians. No need to prepare. Just speak from the heart."

Wayne could tell it was important to the young man, so he thought a moment, cleared his throat, and said, "It's cold out here, eh?"

Amos shook his head. "This vast mystery and that's all I get. Everyone knows space is cold and dark."

Wayne looked through the visor at Amos. "It's not really dark, though. It's just that there's not a lot for the light to reflect off of."

"Howah," Amos laughed. "Now that's profound!"

The two bobbed at the end of their lines for a long moment. Amos raised his hand to shield his eyes and looked off toward the horizon, only there was no horizon to look off towards. He turned to Wayne. "It's tough to be an Indian with no horizon."

Wayne couldn't see Amos's face behind the visor and so couldn't tell if he was being sarcastic or serious. "You need some coffee, space cadet." He grabbed the tether line and began to pull himself back to the ship. "*Pezutasapa*." In Dakota, coffee was "black medicine."

"*Makade-mashkikiwaaboo*." Amos liked the sound of the Anishinaabe-mowin word better. "Black water medicine," he translated.

Wayne nodded. "Either way it's what you need." He smiled that way he did. "Good strong coffee."

Drunk Camp

Late afternoon was his morning today, and it was a grim headache. He eyed their camp blearily, looking for her. Their meager things were stuffed in plastic grocery bags, scattered around the nest they'd made in a stand of sumac by the river.

Where was she?

His head rang, the light too bright on the water. *Gichi-ziibi*; what the old ones called the big river. Mississippi now. He sat, and pushed himself up onto the rock near where he'd passed out, and reached down for last night's bottle.

Cars buzzed across the bridge above, heading wherever it was that people went. Work? Home? It made little difference. Escape was what all that movement was about, escape from those things that made you crazy, that threatened you. A bottle in the bush seemed like escape. Their camp at the river too, and those people in their cars didn't know it, maybe didn't know empty bottles, but they lived empty too. Their movement their disease. Running from something, running toward something; running always.

Like the men who paid him, who liked his smooth cheeks and the way his long hair hid his face; the men he emptied. They longed for something, they all did, but their escape was only a spasm, a thin white rope of release, and a quick retreat. Pleasure was fleeting, longing was lasting. The city sped by above.

Where had she gone?

It was too much to yell her name, would hurt his head too much in this light, so he just threw the empty bottle at a tree. Plastic only bounced when it hit; he missed the shatter of glass, the sound so beautiful, each tinkling shard a fragment of the broken world falling away—but glass vodka was too much. It had long ago stopped being a pleasure. Longed for, sure, but too much. Too fleeting for what it cost him.

He ached for it now, for her as well. Where would she go without him? Her coming back would be good—she knew broken pieces. Even if she was no better at picking them up than he was, it was good to be with someone who understood the sound of breaking glass. But until then another bottle would be enough. She longed for it as much as he did. He'd make sure to have it here when she came back.

Five bucks, ten—he'd wash his hands and rinse his hair in the river later, but only after a trip to the liquor store. They didn't judge him or what he did, they couldn't, not really. Plastic vodka and a stumble back to camp. It was how they made their money.

She'd be back then he knew. Waiting, longing—if not for him, then for what he could give her. The bottle wouldn't be full for long. Their pain would draw away as they tilted their heads back, as he did now, the walk to camp done. Back on his rock, he worked on the bottle, her bags still scattered around the area, just as he'd left them hours ago, but still no her. He thought her name, sent it flying out over the water, as he pressed the bottle to his lips again. He slipped from his seat, sat on the long grass they'd flattened in this nest of sumac, and leaned his head back on the rock and looked up at the murals unfolding in the radio static that gathered above the river every night.

He knew you couldn't see the radio static the way you saw the trees and the bridge, or heard the cars above, but he knew too it was real. It was like the manidoog, the spirits everyone used to know. Radio waves agitated the air and when he looked up at that static there in the twilit sky, he could see what everyone else overlooked. He saw his life.

Tonight he saw those days at the sugar bush, tending the fires, boiling the maple sap into syrup and then working it into sugar, drilling the trunks with Uncle and setting the taps; draining winter from the trees. Time ran kind of backwards in the static, as if it were wound differently there. He watched the old man in the sky and marveled now, as he did then, at the ease with which Uncle did those hard tasks. He raised the bottle to the old one up there and took a drink. The image began to move away from him, turning red as it did, taillights receding over a distant rise and dropping suddenly out of view.

He took another drink, smaller this time, and thought about Uncle and looked at the static above the water. It never showed him the ugliness of what he did for these bottles, nor did he see the loneliness of the men who paid him, nor the ways he had failed those he cared for—like her. He preferred not to think about it and looked up again into the static and saw his cousins sprawled on a blanket one night at the Sisseton powwow, his five-year-old self right in the middle of them. Too tired to crawl into the tent, the three of them just flopped down on their backs and watched the fireflies pulsing above. As he drifted towards sleep that night the fireflies and the stars began to fade into one another, the fireflies floating off into the depths of space and the stars dropping down so he could almost touch them.

He took another drink as he watched this moment and willed his younger self to stand up, because he knew if he did, if he rose at just the right moment, his body would be drawn to the stars and he would lift off into the sky like an astronaut, until he was nothing more than a tiny pulsing light. People would think he was just a firefly or a distant star, and maybe she would still be here, he thought, if I were gone. He drank some more, and then again, their young bodies still at rest on the blanket, and again he drank, no one rising to the stars, swallowing more and more until the static dropped down out of the sky and his memories drowned in the buzz of it. He nodded off, head propped on the rock, facing the river, the bottle tipped in the long grass.

Moments later, or maybe it was hours, he couldn't tell, and didn't think it much mattered, he opened his eyes to the now dark night above the water. The static had run off. It must've been hours if his head had cleared this much. The dark didn't hurt his eyes; the dark made things clear.

He heard a stirring in the shallows at the edge of the river—a beaver maybe, or a raccoon? Something moving in the water along the beach. One day he knew the sun would swell up, reach for the earth, and that sand at the river's edge would fuse into bottle glass that would never break, but would hiss and pulse until it evaporated and became a part of the dying star, just as a drunk becomes a part of the bottle consuming him.

Leaning forward, he peered through the twisted antlers of the sumac branches. The sloshing stopped, but now he heard steps on the sand and saw something hazy and soft at the edges there. Her he hoped.

She walked up the path they had cut from their nest to the river, pale and shimmering in the dark, blonde hair drab as always and her skin leathered from living too long on the streets and too many cigarettes when she could bum them off the men who sought him out.

Her red hoodie, faded to a dull pink, was still mud-stained, but now was heavy with the water that drained from her form as she moved toward him. He could hear the drops patter on the ground, little fragments of the river falling into their camp. She cried silently; he could tell from the way her shoulders shook that she was weeping. Her chin had fallen toward her chest, her face hidden in the shadow of her hair.

Then last night came back to him and he wanted to remember that he had no idea why she left camp, but really he remembered her jostling him and him shoving her away with a grunt. She had wanted something and he pushed her away. Her words were lost in the slur of the night's bottle. She had wanted help and he failed her.

"Here," he said as she walked by, offering her the bottle, even though he knew she wouldn't stop. She longed for something different now. He watched as she glimmered up the path, a flickering pink light under the dark trees. He would help her now. He'd made a mistake; he'd bring her back to their nest, and she could take care of him like she always did. She would take care of him, it was what she did. He tipped the bottle back against his lips, but there was hardly anything left there. It was empty, spent. He tossed it away.

He followed as she made her way up the path from their camp below to the bridge above. He tried to catch up to her, but couldn't, even when he ran. He was sure she'd come back to him, if only he could reach her in time, but then on the bridge he saw she was uncertain in the grim yellow light from the street lamp. He could see through her. She was mist and she never stopped crying, her shoulders still shaking. She never even looked back at him, just walked to the railing, kicked off her shoes, and climbed on top of it. The harder she cried the less distinct she became; her tears consumed what was left of her.

He approached as quickly as he dared. He didn't want to frighten her. She was looking down at the river churning blackly below. He looked over the railing as well and saw the stars captured in that dark water. She shifted, still weeping, and suddenly slipped over the edge. He leaned over the railing to grab for her, but she was already gone. A wisp of mist hung there, sparkling in the air. He stretched his hand out to it, to the stars he saw beyond it, flickering like fireflies at the tips of his fingers, then lost his balance and became an astronaut, drifting weightless between the stars down there for a moment that stretched into an eternity of black water.

Fiona looked out the window at the clear summer sky. The blue there stood in stark contrast to the shimmering stars in the dark night water. She wondered if her grandpa knew that man who fell? Or had he watched? Maybe he tried to stop him?

She caught her breath as a horrible thought struck her. Since he had wandered off into a swamp on a cold January night, did Grandpa believe he was that falling man? Was he suicidal?

She shook her head to clear the thought from her mind, but she couldn't. In health class, they learned that suicidal people often gave their things away. Grandpa had given the stories to Jimmy—left them in his care. They also often wrote letters or posted messages on their accounts explaining why they were so unhappy, even if they might not speak directly about killing themselves. There was something depressing or dark—or kind of melancholy, she thought recalling one of her vocab words—on every page he wrote; something sad or angry or disappointed about what the world looked like. Was this package she got a long, long suicide note?

Mom would say he should be sad and disappointed for how he treated them, Fiona thought, and should be angry at himself and no one else, because he had done it to himself. "And no amount of writing will make that better," Fiona could imagine Mom saying as she took the pages and stuffed them in a paper sack before taking them away.

Fiona whisked open her camera again and took pictures of the pages she'd just read. As she framed the last page its final sentence caught her eye. A man falling while stretching his hands out to the stars at his fingertips. "Falling isn't what he's doing," she said as she clicked her phone off. "He's reaching for something," she said as she picked up the envelope addressed "To: the Grandchild." "At least I hope he was."

Fiona fingered the taped-over seal on the envelope, worried that she might find something that confirmed her worst fears inside. What if it was a suicide note? The thought frightened her. She drew a breath and counted to ten—Mom said it was the best thing to do if you felt your emotions getting away from you. She exhaled, considered setting the envelope aside, and then slid her finger under the tape. Waiting wouldn't change whatever Grandpa said in the letter. It had been sitting sealed up for eighteen years.

Noozis,

So I don't risk forgetting it, let me start here: Never forget we're Anishinaabe. Your mother probably doesn't care to remember, and if that's because of how I lived, then so be it. She's lost to it, perhaps, but you don't need to be, noozis. The old ones always look out for us, those grandmothers and grandfathers that came before we did. Even if we may not always see them, they see us. They see your mother, they see you; they care for you and you should care for them. Let these words help you remember that if you ever feel lost. Your mother probably wouldn't listen to me at this point in her life, but my words will help her as well, should she want it.

I don't think I'm ever meant to see you, so I won't be able to tell you that "noozis" means grandchild. My lungs ache all the time now. I can't even yell at this fool dog who found me wandering the streets. She's my only company here at my camp on the Mississippi.

Sounds romantic, doesn't it? Camping on the river. A dog. A man. Alone. A dream.

It's not all that romantic really. I'm not off in some pristine corner of the wilderness as I write this letter for you. I'm in Minneapolis. I summer here and when winter comes I work my way up to northern Minnesota where I'll find a nice cabin to stay in. The city's good in the summer. Ways to make a little money doing odd jobs here and there. Work by day, stay at the river at night. No rent, no hassles, savings for the long winter. I was working in a produce warehouse until a few weeks ago, but they let me go when they found me sleeping behind a pallet of grapes that had come in from California.

I didn't mean to fall asleep, but these lungs. Just breathing wears me out. I guess that's why I don't think I'll ever see you. You haven't been born yet, but you will be—and then you will be born again and again. Not literally, but in spirit. You'll be like me, always moving toward something, some kind of knowledge about the world, about the pain and loneliness in it, and the love, too—and the strangeness of it. Learning, too, about who we are and who our ancestors are. You'll want to move toward what your mother surely ignores, and what I can only ever imperfectly grasp. You're like me, I'm bequeathing that to you across this stretch of time, bequeathing it with this letter and these stories: you want to make sense out of that face in the mirror. That young Anishinaabe person standing there, whose face is yours, whose hair is yours, whose eyes see you, but cannot clearly see what Anishinaabe is. All we have is our experience to guide us toward that, and ours—yours and mine—is a lack of experience. Our family history has seen to that.

Our experience as Anishinaabe is this: your great-grandfather, my dad—Dewey was his English name—was raised on the reservation, sent to boarding school by parents who didn't have the money to feed him and his four brothers. They sent the boys to the school so they could eat, not thinking about the pain of separation. Our separation from our ancestors starts with theirs from their family. Dad ran away from that school at age fifteen, but never went home—he never said why, either, and you'll learn in a bit why I was not able to ask him. He went to work on the railroad, then became a lumberman, then went to load ore on the ships in Duluth or Superior—I suppose it depended on if he was in a Minnesota mood or a Wisconsin one at any given time. In Duluth he met and married my mother, another Rose. The First Rose. I'm sure your mother has told you about my Rose, my wife, your grandma. The Second Rose. She and your mom were so close I wouldn't be surprised if your name, if you are a girl, is Third Rose.

"Half-right," Fiona mumbled, thinking about her middle name, as she tracked his story—their story—through the neat little letters inked on the whisper-thin onionskin paper of his letter.

Your great-grandfather Dewey was forty-one when he married my mother Rose in 1928 and nearly another ten years passed until I was born in 1937. Their only child. My mother Rose died when I was seven and Dad started working on the ore boats then, not just loading them, but clambering aboard and drifting away over Lake Superior—gichigami is what we call it in Anishinaabe. He always left me in the care of one or another of the wives of his fellow crew members. Since he was gone nearly all the time, I grew up with a dozen different brothers and sisters, none of whom shared our blood. Some were dark-haired and dark-complected like we are, my grandchild—I can see in my mind's eye your resemblance to me—but unlike you and I, these families that took me in were Italian, Jewish, and Slovenian. Perhaps I was darker than many of my mothers and their other children, but I was close enough. My mother, First Rose, was a fair-haired daughter of a Norwegian, the Duluth city assessor, and my skin tone would lighten some in the winter. I think that helped. Their children and I were similar enough that I could be passed off as a cousin, and I was only ever rarely introduced as "the little Indian boy."

This is all to say that by the time I reached high school I hardly knew the old man. Your great-grandpa's work on the ore boats dried up then, but not because of his age. He was still strong as a bull—a bigger person than we are, grandchild—broad-shouldered and barrel-chested, but his mind had begun to wander. Dementia, Alzheimer's, something else—I'm not sure, but those names are just names and they wouldn't change the fact that he couldn't care for himself. We bought a place outside Duluth, up on the North Shore, near one of the many little rivers that tumble down to the big lake, gichigami, and I became the parent to my father . . .

I'm getting a little off the trail of where I wanted this letter to go, noozis. Rather than telling our story, I wanted to talk more about how to see our story. Let me start over.

No, Fiona thought.

Then she thought it again, only this time said it aloud. "No."

She added, "This is where I need the letter to go." She hoped her grandfather's spirit, even if only nearly mature, might hear. "Mom's never told me these sorts of things." It then occurred to Fiona that perhaps Mom had never heard them either.

Since being fired from the job at the produce warehouse I have a lot of time to write, so I could work and rework this letter to death—which is what I usually do when I write, but I won't this time. Last year I would've thrown that story about Dad away. I'd have torn up the letter and started over when I lost the trail, but not this year. Maybe it's a story you'll find interesting, so I'll just leave it there. Other pages I've written elsewhere touch on Dewey's life, so you'll see him again. Be patient.

This new writing method—of not working it to death—is something I learned from that stray I'm camping with. This fool dog—she's a little mutt with a recessive gene that gives her a green eye—has a keen perception of what life is stirring in the brush around her and that's taught me to live like her, in the moment. See, she can hear a squirrel skittering through the underbrush and before it even knows she's there, she's killed it. See a squirrel, catch a squirrel. That's my method now, too: think about you, write for you. I'm working on this letter because death hears me skittering in the underbrush and I don't want it to get me before I've told you what you need to know about these stories.

Death, Fiona thought. Not suicide.

I call this little mutt Misaabe—you can pronounce that Mi-sah-bay. It's our Anishinaabe word for Bigfoot, the giant being in the forest. She's a little dog, but like the giant man she comes to help Anishinaabe when they need it. I should say, when I needed it. Misaabe, the giant, not the dog, finds Anishinaabe when they're lost in the woods. If one of we Anishinaabe gets lost when we're out searching for medicine—by which, I mean the plants and herbs by which our bodies and minds can be brought back to a harmonious balance—Misaabe finds us and sets us on the right trail. You shouldn't be afraid of him if you're lost and doing a good thing. He's shy and keeps to himself, until one of us needs help—and that brings me to the dog.

After getting fired I retreated to my camp, whiling the days away by myself, fretting over the stories, changing a word here and there. Sometimes I'd head up onto the streets to chase down a can of beans or a jar of instant coffee when I needed them.

Other than those trips after food, my contact with others was limited. Being alone then was a lot like being lost, I now realize. I spent, and still spend, a lot of my life alone, but am not lost since Misaabe found me.

Returning from one of my forays to buy beans, Misaabe spotted me as I headed down to the river, and she came running, nosed me like she knew me—strange behavior for a stray—so I knelt and petted her. She had no collar and her stink made my eyes water. "No home?" I asked. She bolted from the sidewalk and down the path in the woods, headed for my camp. Fast friends ever since, but she didn't get in my tent until I thoroughly scrubbed her with Dial soap—one thing your mom may not ever mention is you won't get warts if you use Dial soap. It's also pretty good at taming the stink of a stray mutt.

Since Misaabe found me, the woods here are filled with the ghosts of squirrels, moles, and raccoons that she has chased down and, generally, cleanly dispatched with a quick violent shake that snaps her victims' necks. The woods run with the spirit of near misses as well, the still-living squirrels, deer, and coyotes that have evaded Misaabe's sometimes overly ambitious attacks. She's that kind of hunter. Honest in her love of it.

The woods that run with these spirits of the still-living and the quickly dead line the bluffs along the Mississippi River where it runs through the city. They are a narrow band of trees, brush, and limestone outcroppings that seemingly separate the streets above from the water below. Some people might see these woods as a place to step out of the world of pavement, buildings, and bridges; they might see them as a place to escape into the realm of falling leaves, sighing winds, and eagle, fox, and coyote sightings—but they really aren't an escape. The woods aren't a threshold you can step over, nor are they a door you can shut against the noise of that world of cars and streets and people, family included. They're all still there in the woods. All of them. The bridge over the water, arching high above the treetops, buzzes with cars and trucks, and planes draw white lines across the sky even farther above. Discarded condoms and broken fishing rods line the riverbank, and so do the eagle-torn carcasses of bullheads—evidence that there are other lives in the woods, even the lives of the no longer living. Every night a ghost couple drippingly staggers out of the river, and they noisily sort through the empty booze bottles scattered around the abandoned drunk camp upstream from me. They drain those empties of ghost vodka, their addiction unquiet even in death. While I wonder how their last days went, I don't think I need to wonder what killed them.

Fiona sighed, relieved. Grandpa had not known the falling man, but he knew his ghost. She was sure this meant he didn't see himself as a falling man, either. She hoped that was what it meant.

Your mother and Grandma Rose are here, too, constant in my mind, and the river aches with the same chemical pain as my lungs. Carp gasp at the shoreline, their breath as labored as mine.

You are here among these trees as well, noozis, down here with Misaabe and me. I call you here with my words. I see you as I write. Your bright smile, the gleam in your eyes.

These woods don't separate us from the world is what I'm trying to convey here, nor do these stories I share with you. They are a place where things come together, but not always in ways that others would recognize as harmonious. Sometimes it's terrible to be a squirrel, a bullhead, or a ghost at the other end of a dog, an eagle, or a bottle, but there is a terrible beauty in the world as well as a loving beauty, you'd best remember that. Both are beautiful because that is how they are—and how we are. How our story is. They're harmonious, but not in the way most people think of harmony.

We are like the woods, noozis—harmonious in this other way. We are mixed up, a place where things we don't always understand come together—sometimes terribly and sometimes lovingly. You and I are the descendants of Anishinaabe and French people, and thus of the priests and medicine people who described how the world worked to our ancestors. It's easier for most people to pretend things are divided rather than connected—just as your mother pretends she and I are divided. For most people it's easier, and less risky, to see the differences in things rather than the similarities between them. It's easier to think that the city and the woods, Anishinaabe and White, and priest and medicine man differ from one another—rather than seeing the ways they join along the river. I wish your mother could see that, could see that Anishinaabe is a good way, even if I wasn't. She's divided herself—and you—from that, because of me. Just as I can see you in my mind's eye, I can see she neglects how our ancestors shape our lives. She thinks that by ignoring them, she will keep me out of your life, spare you the pain I gave her and your grandma. She thinks that you are not me because I am dead, but you and I touch one another through the words on a piece of paper. We understand one another. I summon you when I summon these words. In this other sort of harmony you can feel what moved me to write for you. Not the pain your mother feels, but the pain of separation—and the desire for connection—that I feel.

Fiona looked up from the letter. The words were packed so tightly on the page that her eyes needed a rest. She glanced at the window just as a crow tipped its wings like it was waving at her. A pale sliver of daylight moon hung in the sky far above that bird's dipping wings. Her house was not even ten miles from Minneapolis and the river where her grandfather camped. She thought he must have seen this same pale moon on the day he wrote the letter eighteen years ago. Probably saw it hanging just there, above the river.

She smoothed the paper against her knee and continued reading.

Since I am dead now, there's no sense in not saying it: I was not a good man for your mom and grandma. I was not a good man at all, and still am not—except when I'm alone here at the river. The only good thing I have is words, but that's what makes me bad as well. Until four or five years ago I made a living lying to people. I'd charm them with outlandish tales, gain their trust, and then take their money—never enough to wipe them out, but enough to feed, house, and clothe your mom and grandma, while withholding enough, often even most of it, for myself, the things I wanted. I conned and I gambled and your grandma, my Rose, still loved me. She was an improver—thought she could improve me, turn me around, set me on the right track, even after we'd been together twelve years and I still hadn't worked an honest day in my life. It worried her, caretaker that she was—she lost sleep that I never did, fretting about where the money came from and the people I associated with. Her guts were so knotted with worry for so long that the knots became cancer. I made her sick. I gave her that disease and I left so she could get better. The one good thing I could do for my family was to leave them.

See, I couldn't stand to give her any more pain. When we were together, her love was always unconditional, but it was stretched thin with anxiety. I knew she'd suffer some sort of devastation from my abandonment, but I knew her love for your mother would eventually overcome that pain. I know she was heartbroken when I left—my departure was a symbol of her failure to reset my path, but I knew, too, she'd rally past any pain I'd left behind. With me gone, she could worry about herself and your mother, take care of her health rather than try to take care of her husband. I saw no sense in her wasting any more vital energy on me. I was on a trail that had been decided long before I met her. I didn't want to be reset. Still don't. Can't.

But I can ease the pain of separation—I hope—with my stories. They're all here. I dreamed them for you. Dreams tell different sorts of truths than facts do; facts are the dreams of unimaginative people. You won't find out what I've been doing in the decades since I left my Rose and your mother—well, you know I worked at a produce warehouse and camp at the river with a smelly mutt. I will add that I've never seen Misaabe—the giant, not the mutt—in real life, never clapped my eyes on him or sensed his looming presence, but he does come to me in my dreams and speak to me. I write his words down when that happens and have included them with these other stories. He speaks gruffly, and you can tell English is not his accustomed language, but he has much to say that I agree with. He feels people have lost their way in the world and he wants to help them find new ways to see their lives. He tells people how to live through my dreams; he tries to set them back on a track they stepped off long ago.

Anishinaabe uphold Misaabe as a symbol of honesty, you might say—honesty as a virtue, a deep and guiding principle. Unlike me, he lives by the heart and speaks from the heart. I always speak from the craftiest part of the brain, but he lives to remind us to be honest to the earth and the living beings and spirits here—and to be honest to others, like you. I can't be honest with anyone, but my stories are honestly for you.

We know Misaabe lives in the woods, and though I dream of seeing him, he eludes me because I find it too hard to be as honest with myself as he is with himself. Honesty is elusive. He is always just out of my sight, until I close my eyes. I live in the harmony of such contrariness—seeing things with closed eyes, telling you true things with stories I make up. This contrariness is the woods in the city, noozis. Is the Anishinaabe in you. It's us. Separated by all these years, by lies, by death, but, though apart, still together in these words. I spoke each one of them aloud as I wrote them down. I hope you can hear my voice as you read along.

My love for you,

Mishomis (Grandpa)

While she had glimpsed Grandpa's hand writing the words before she read them, Fiona had yet to hear his voice coming up off the paper and into her head. She didn't know if his voice was high or low, or if it was raspy or clear. He complained of his lungs a lot, so maybe his voice had that sort of watery gurgling sound she got when a cold in its final stages settled in her chest. That sort of voice always made her feel good. She knew it meant she was getting better.

Even if Fiona couldn't hear her grandpa, the dark rumble of Misaabe's voice sounded in her head as she read his thoughts. It started somewhere deep in the center of his body and just sort of slowly rose up from there until it boomed out of his mouth into the forest and her grandpa's dreams. The shows on TV about Bigfoot never really got any good footage of what he looked like, but they often recorded his voice deep in the night, always from the other side of a valley or across a lake it seemed, and it rumbled through the trees like the voice she heard when she read what he told Grandpa.

She guessed, too, from Grandpa's letter that Misaabe's voice was sort of sharp and shrill—Misaabe the mutt, not the giant. Like the giant she was honest, though. In Fiona's experience, dogs never lied. They either liked you or didn't and they never tried to deny their feelings or keep them from you. For some reason that dog of his, which she pictured as being some sort of wiry terrier mutt with long legs and fur so gray it was almost silver, loved her grandpa, and knew it the moment she saw him. He might have thought being a scammer made him unlovable, but Misaabe found him otherwise. Fiona smiled.

She loved all this—she wasn't sure what to call it—information about Misaabe. Or was it a story about him? Or from him? Both, maybe? It didn't matter because she loved his giant heart and that he wanted people to connect back to the woods and the water and the leaves where he lived. She loved that mutt, too, without ever seeing her, just because she was willing to connect with a lonely old man. Misaabe just wants us to be honest and see what we have, she thought. Without those things we're lost.

Her grandpa was honest in his love for her, she was certain of that, even if he had only ever imagined who she was, and Misaabe was honest in her love for him. Her grandpa's stories might share only a few of the facts of his life with her, but they gave her something else. Something that made sense in that harmonious way he talked about, where you close your eyes to see what's not there in front of you. When he closed his eyes, her grandpa saw Misaabe, but opening them saw nothing. He sounded disappointed when he wrote that he'd never seen a Sasquatch. Like he thought something was missing in his life, something more than a giant. Me? she wondered. Mom? Us, his family?

"Maybe I should show this letter to her," Fiona mumbled, thinking of her mom. She looked up at the closed door of her room. Maybe Mom'd be able to hear her father's voice there, his disappointment. It painted a different picture of the man than what Fiona saw in the picture Mom kept hidden. This one in the letter was not so gleaming and mischievous as that one in the picture. Maybe Mom would be able to hear that in his voice. Maybe she'd hear a man who worried about *not* seeing Misaabe and about his lack of honesty. Maybe she'd hear a man who worried about not seeing his child and grandchild, rather than just seeing the laughing man in the picture who ran out on his wife and daughter. That would still make Mom mad, him saying the best thing he could do was leave his Rose when she was sick with cancer—Fiona thought it a bad thing, too, like poaching and squatting. Frowning, Fiona stared at the letter. He had made up a reason about leaving his wife and daughter to make himself feel better for what he did. She wasn't sure it was a good one. It was trying too hard. If not a lie, it was something other than honest—even if he really believed it.

What he'd done had hurt Mom and Grandma, leaving them to care for themselves and going off to live his own life. As far as Fiona knew he'd never contacted them again.

A thought popped to mind. A line in the letter. She worked her way back through the last few paragraphs until she found it. That line about getting enough money so that Mom and Grandma would have food and a place to live. It could mean he continued to send money after he left. The way he wrote that line made it hard to see if it was only before he left or if it included after as well. She could ask Mom about that, if she decided to share the letter. Knowing he had provided something, even if he was otherwise gone from their lives, meant he wanted to take some sort of responsibility for them. Meant he tried to maintain some sort of connection. Meant he cared, maybe.

Fiona flipped the last page of the letter over and found a glossary on the back. *Anishinaabe Words,* he'd written at the top and under that added, *these will help you understand.* Below that were two columns, one labeled *Anishinaabemowin* and the other *English.* There he'd written the word for coffee, and those for dog, horse, and deer. She saw the words for grandmother and moon, for river. He included the word for flying snakes that he said swoop through the forest at night as well as the word for the stick you use against them. He'd written the words for crow, canoe, and story, as well as those for stars, astronaut, and spaceship. Next to some of the words, he'd written little notes—instructions for how to hold the stick as the snakes flew by, an explanation of why the word for moon and grandmother was the same, that kind of thing.

For a few minutes Fiona skimmed over the list and those notes. She tried to sound the words out, but they were difficult and she knew there was little chance of pronouncing them right, and that question about whether Grandpa continued sending Mom and Grandma money after he left, kept distracting her from her efforts.

She wanted to believe the best of him, but it was difficult not to think the worst. He told me he was crafty, she thought. That mischievous smile in the sock drawer popped to mind. But what does he want from me?

She took photos of the letter before setting it aside. As she reached for the stories, it struck her. He knows Mom's angry, or at least guesses that she is, because who wouldn't be? He sent the stories and letter to me because he wants me to tell her about him. Wants me to show her that he was still thinking about us at the end of his life, that he did something other than lie and leave. He wrote stories. He cared for a dog—or, really, the letter showed that a dog cared for him. That he wasn't so bad. He wants me to help clean up the mess he made. Knowing Mom's feelings, she wasn't sure if she wanted that job.

"Haven't you ever just heard of telling the truth?" she said, before remembering that he said he couldn't be that honest.

Frustrated with where her thoughts were leading, she took the pages of the stories—the ones she'd already read—and put them on the bottom of the ones she was about to read. His stories were better than thinking about his life.

Indians in Space, Episode Two: Event Horizon

Wayne and Amos had orbited the black hole for the better part of a week. Amos monitored it with scientific instruments and Wayne did the same with his eyes through the window—only there was nothing to see. It really is a black hole, Wayne thought. But it sure distorts the starfield around it in interesting ways.

On the fifth day Amos told Wayne, "I've been monitoring the Hawking radiation coming off that old one out there."

Wayne looked to where the black hole was, and wasn't. "What's Hawking radiation?"

"Particles trapped inside the black hole are continually trying to escape from it," Amos explained. "While most are drawn back in by the hole's massive gravity, some are pushed away. They escape. Eventually enough escape and the black hole evaporates." He slowly shook his head. "I've been plotting the Hawking emissions since we got here."

"And?"

"It's strange, it has become very orderly."

"Things are orderly, Amos."

"This is different. It's a higher order of organization. There is too much complex variation in the emissions to be explained by gravitational theory or random chance." He pulled a series of graphs up on the screen above the console. "I've animated a time-lapse scroll through the bars. Watch."

Amos pressed a button and the lines rose and fell, pulsing through phases that Wayne could see formed coherent visual phrases that were repeated in complex patterns that had a cadence.

"I noticed the pattern yesterday and it seemed like something I should know. Couldn't put my finger on it though. Until I turned in."

Wayne looked at the young man.

"I was thinking about the bars, about their rhythm as I drifted off to sleep. I began to dream and as I dreamed the bars became a song, with words I knew."

Wayne saw Amos's eyes had grown sad.

"The words were my grandfather's." Amos took a breath, composed himself. "We were all gathered around his bed when he was dying. He was weak and his left hand gently tapped a rhythm against his leg." Amos drummed his fingers softly on the console. "He began to sing and he cycled through the words four times, struggling to keep his breathing tied to the rhythm. It took everything he had. His lips were so dry I thought they were going to crack." Amos looked up into Wayne's face. "He smiled when he finished and just kept smiling at us all night, drifting in and out of dreams. His eyes began to water when the new day dawned and he drew a big breath. The rattle in his chest was unmistakable. He began to tap that rhythm on the blanket again, weakly though, and he opened his mouth, but no words came out."

Amos's eyes grew moist.

"Uncle began to sing the words Grandfather had sung. Then I joined in, and my cousins too. He didn't have the breath for it so we sang for him. We sang him on that journey." Amos drifted to the window where he stared toward the point where there was no light. He took a deep breath and faced Wayne. "It's dying. It's singing that final song."

Wayne floated to the young man's side. "It's good you were there for your grandfather, space cadet. He taught you many things that day, including how to listen to that old one out there." Wayne looked where the light wasn't and then asked, "How much time does it have?"

"It's sung through nearly two times since the rhythm emerged four days ago. That means two more times through, so I expect another four, maybe five days."

"Have you reported this to NASA?"

"Ours or theirs?"

"Ours." Wayne smiled. *Native American Space Adventuring.* He grinned every time he thought about the name the Native nations had chosen for their space program.

"I haven't reported anything," Amos said. He looked at Wayne. "Should I tell theirs too?"

"They'll be interested in your data on the Hawking emissions and your prediction about its passing."

Both men returned their attention to the black hole, looking toward the event horizon.

"What about our NASA?" Amos asked. "Won't they want to know?"

"I think we should head back and tell them," Wayne said. "They'll be interested in these things you've learned. It confirms what the old ones always say about the world and the Great Mystery." Wayne smiled that gentle way he did. "It's all alive."

The event horizon they now knew was a diaphragm from which song pushed forth. "Everything has a song," Wayne said. "Sometimes we just need to learn how to listen."

Amos nodded, but he already knew that.

Feathertruth

Take that feather, men, find it there at the root of that tree, and take it in them stub fingers. See me, men, take it as I do. Make big fingers small, make stub fingers fine. Like this, men, like me.

Listen!

Softly touch it and raise it from that tree root to your dull snout, men, and draw the smell of it in. Like this, like so. Draw deep, men, only not too deep. Like me, softly.

Listen.

You say it smells of sky, men, of wheeling birds on the wing. Yes, men, yes! Birds must wheel in the sky.

You say it smells like a million bird generations of sky flight. Yes, men, yes!

You say it smells like that angel you find in them words of men? Men, that one soaring in warm sun, rising from the words of men and away from the earth? Men. I shake my head. I bare my teeth and knock fallen branch against sturdy tree. And knock again. And again I holler at the treeline. No, men, no!

Listen men!

Smell that feather as it is, not as you wish it were. Don't mistake them words of men for that feather truth. Draw deep, men.

Does that feather smell of the tree, men? Smell it! Does it smell of bird desire?

That feather smells of bird dreams of the earth, men, of the home-ground, not of angels. Leave the words of men, men; leave them.

That feather smells of sky and earth, men, of that wheeling freedom and that warm ground that accepts my footprints. You see them, men, but you don't see me; you smell the sky, men, but you forget the earth.

Draw deep and think, men.

What does that bird desire in the tree? Can you smell it in that feather? I smell grounding, men, that's what that bird desires. Home-ground is what that bird seeks, a nest in the branch, men, a tree life with roots.

The bird plants its feather at the root of that tree, men. That bird hopes that feather is a magnet, men. That bird hopes, men, but that bird wheels away, drawn to fly as it must. Desire is no match for instinct, men, but that wheeling bird hopes to be drawn back to the root, men, to that feather, and one day it falls, men, and that bird dies, and when it does, men, it can rest in the roots. Grounded in the warm earth, men. That bird desires what that angel flies away from.

Put that feather back, men, softly, there at the root. Listen. Don't let bird dreams wheel away.

Tree Desire

What if a man were a tree, men, what would that tree desire in the bird? Wings, men, feathers?

Leaves, men, are the feathers on the wings of the tree. And a tree who was a man, men, would pull its roots from the homeground and become bird, men, bark on the wing, leaves in the sky.

Listen!

Leaf wings of tree men swirl up in the whirlwind, men, and rise to those places that tree men can only dream, men. The clouds, men, the clouds that nourish them. Trees take wing in tree men dreams, men, tree branches the wings for angel feather leaves and then, men, them clouds become the dream you rise to, men, the tree men heaven.

Leave it men! Leave the clouds found in the words of men; men, leave that heaven.

Listen!

Men should not make trees into men, men. Men should not make clouds into heaven, or leaves into wings, men. Let the tree be, men, let leaves be leaves, and let the tree find its heaven, men, when it falls to the homeground. Men, stop being angels, stop making trees live in cloud heaven. Become the tree, men, as the tree is. Fall to the earth, men, don't rise from it.

Kneel There

Rain falls onto our bodies, men, them drops fall from our hair; from my long arm, from your stub hands, men, they tumble. Them drops fall to the homeground, men, they feed it. That's water, men.

Them drops, men, that rain, runs from our bodies, men, runs over ground; runs to creek, runs to river, runs to lake, men. We are water, men; our blood is water; our blood runs. Our bodies are a pulsing river, men; our bodies a muddy lake. Murky water, men, that's us. Scratch chin, men, rub stub hands. Wonder, men. Think rain!

Take it in, men. Water yourselves. Water, yourselves. Bend to creek, bend to river. Kneel, men. Kneel there, not elsewhere!

See me scoop creek to mouth, men, feed the river. See me! Scoop river to mouth, men, feed the muddy lake. See me rise, men, fed with rain. See me step long, men; see me turn to water deep in the trees; see my step melt into the homeground, men. See me escape your measure.

Water beats into the homeground through my steps, men, and water beats through the veins of the trees, rising up, men, blood rising to the sky in bursts of green leaf clouds.

Listen, men. Them treeleaves are green water. Drink them in. See them turn to rain; them leaves breathe water, men; their blood rises to the sky and their spent bodies tumble to the homeground, men. Food for the earth.

Turn to rain, men; make for the sky. Let the leaves of your waterspent bodies tumble down to the homeground, men. Spent leaf men feed the earth!

Fiona smiled thinking about Misaabe telling men to kneel elsewhere and stop being angels. It made her think of that photo of her mischievous Grandpa on his wedding day. She knew he was grinning so hugely because he'd refused a church wedding. Misaabe saw no need for churches and angels, either. Neither did she. Mom had made her go to Sunday school and confirmation classes with Dane, but when she said she was quitting, Mom didn't put up any sort of fuss. She never went to church so it would be hard to insist that Fiona needed to stick with it. Church didn't have much to offer, Fiona thought. That's something Mom and I agree on. Mom must've gone to church as a kid, though. She never said anything about it, but she had talked how when Mom was little Grandma had made her pray every night before bed. "I pray the Lord my soul to keep" is all Fiona could remember of that prayer.

When she had asked her mom what that meant, Mom said, "It means you want God to take your soul to heaven so he can take care of you."

When she was little that thought had made Fiona happy. It meant her Grandma was being cared for, just like her mom and dad took care of her. Grandma had believed that sort of thing, Mom told her. It surprised Fiona, now that she thought about it, that Mom didn't seem to. She and Mom and Dad only ever went to church for weddings and funerals, and those were always only Dad's relatives.

Mom loved everything about Grandma Rose so much, yet she didn't go to church like Grandma had. Why, Fiona wondered, but only for a second. It had to be because of Grandma's cancer, her death. Mom's probably angry about that, too, she thought. Both Grandma and Grandpa had left her before she was ready to be on her own. Fiona hated to think of how she'd feel if Mom or Dad suddenly left. The thought left her cold.

Indians in Space, Episode Three: Blue Horizons

Something went wrong on the jump back to Earth. Amos had confirmed their coordinates both pre-jump and post-jump, but as they looked down from orbit half of northern North America was swallowed in water. The blue expanse extended over most of central Canada, reaching from Hudson's Bay deep into Minnesota and the Dakotas.

"We jumped to some other time," Wayne observed. "That's not how home looked when we left."

"The black hole," Amos suggested.

Wayne looked puzzled. "The black hole?"

Amos explained. The warping of space-time at the black hole was profound and as their craft slingshotted out of its orbit, they must have been torn from their familiar temporal continuum and into this one. "But I don't know if we've gone into the past or the future," Amos concluded. He drifted to the window; water could be so beautiful, but he questioned what he saw now.

"Global warming," Amos muttered, turning to look at Wayne. "Our nations are drowned." Amos was sure his home at White Earth and Wayne's at Sisseton were victims of fossil fuels.

Wayne nodded and thought a moment. Finally he said, "It all depends on the water, space cadet."

Now it was Amos's turn to look puzzled.

"I think we'd best go down there and then you'll see." Wayne smiled. "I suppose we'll need to saddle up the pony.

Moments later, both men were strapped into the shuttle pod—the pony—and having picked a wide hole in the clouds below, made their descent, right toward the middle of all that water.

With no land to land on, the pony hovered a few feet above the swell of the water. A platform detached from the bottom of the pod and descended until it nearly touched the peaks of the gentle waves. A ladder lowered from the pony's belly and the adventurers climbed down.

"Cloaking on," Wayne intoned and the pony and its platform blended into the water below and the sky above. Amos had explained that the device somehow worked through the refraction of light, but Wayne just liked having the option.

"I thought we agreed to reserve cloaking for troubling situations," Amos said.

"The way it blocked this view was troubling," Wayne responded. "I guess you've never seen anything like this."

Wayne was right, Amos realized. The older man appeared to be standing on water with the blue sky bursting brightly all around him. Amos thought he looked like the Indian Jesus must have been.

Stepping to the edge of the platform, Wayne and Amos each filled their lungs hugely with fresh air.

"Now, that feels good," Wayne said as he exhaled. He drew deeply again.

"So much better than the recycled air on board." Amos inhaled. The air was better than coffee; he felt reinvigorated. He looked around. The sky spilled away from him on the back of the water no matter which direction he turned. He shielded his eyes against the bright sun and thought about the first spacewalk they had taken. "It's tough to be an Indian with so many horizons," he laughed. Wayne smiled at the young man; the water and air were good.

Still, something unnerved Amos about this planet, this version of their home. His smile faded and he looked to the elder man. "Seriously, though, I don't know where we are."

"You're here, space cadet."

That smile again, Amos thought. "And here is . . . where?" With the sun straight overhead, it was hard to even know which direction they were looking.

"Head south there," Wayne pointed with his lips, "a good long ways and you'll pull up right at Sisseton, though I think it's probably slightly under water there at the moment."

That meant White Earth, slightly to the north and east of Wayne's home, was surely under water as well. Amos didn't like thinking about that, and there was another question to be asked, so he turned back to Wayne. "But, is this the world before we left or after? Past or future?"

"You tell me."

Amos pursed his lips, furrowed his brow, and scanned the horizons around them once more. "The water and sky are clear, so that suggests humanity has either not yet corrupted them, or that humanity has been gone so long that the world has cleansed itself." Amos shook his head; he suspected the latter was more likely. "Global climate change has claimed our nations," he muttered, suddenly bitter.

Wayne said, "Can I suggest something?"

Sometimes Amos found the older man's smile infuriating. "I'm sure you will."

"Take a drink. The water'll tell you what you need to know."

Amos got on his knees and then lay on his belly at the edge of the platform. The olden days warrior of the painting in his grandfather's front room lay on his belly like this, drinking water from a clear spring, his pony at his side, head bent to the water as well. Like the warrior, Amos scooped the water to his mouth with his left hand and tasted it. He grinned and swallowed heartily. "It's sweet." He got to his knees, relieved. "Sweet water means the ice caps haven't melted. Means the oceans haven't flooded the continent." There was water for warriors and their ponies in this world. Amos shook his head. "I should've known." Chagrin blushed his cheeks. "The air doesn't have that salty ocean tang."

Wayne nodded. "So, what's the water tell you?"

"That we're back before our ancestors had a chance to live here. Sisseton's not underwater; it hasn't been born yet."

"See what knowledge comes your way when you listen with your mouth." Wayne laughed. "That's one of the best ways it makes sense."

"Contrarian," Amos mumbled and fell back on his stomach to get some more water.

"It's some of the first water."

Glacial Lake Agassiz Amos had learned in his geology classes.

Wayne lowered himself to one knee—it was getting a little harder to do every year—and scooped a handful of water to his mouth. "That's what we have here. First water." He wiped his mouth with the back of his hand. "It's good for us. Powerful medicine." He looked up at the sky, beyond the blueness there, beyond their ship in orbit, and thanked the Great Mystery. His world was full of magic. The water transformed Amos's anxiety into understanding.

"We'll fill the reserve tanks before we leave," Wayne told the younger man, "and bring as much of this back as we can."

Amos nodded. "I'm going to have to lay in some heavy calculations to get us back. It may take a few days. We'll have to plot this just so, or we might not get back to the right time."

"I think it's simpler than that, space cadet."

"Oh, I see. You've traveled through warped space-time before." Amos looked skeptical.

"You've already done the calculations, or the ship has."

"When was that?"

"On the way here."

"What?"

"The ship's computer records everything, right?"

Amos said nothing, but his eyes said, "Yeah, so?"

"So we have everything we need right there. If we return to the black hole from the exact backwards direction that should launch us back to the exact right time."

"That seems a bit contrary."

"Contrary's good, space cadet. Contrary works." Wayne wiped his damp hands on his jeans. "Once back there we'll just be more careful when we make the jump back home."

"That doesn't seem so contrary."

"Contrary doesn't mean stupid."

Amos had nothing. Words failed him, so he clambered up the ladder into the belly of the pony, Wayne at his heels.

Working the Edge

Still, he kept working the edge of the glass. Working it, working it, pressing antler tine to edge, nipping at it, bits of glass bit off, flecks of green gathering in his palm. Honing that shard of green bottle glass into a point sharp enough to pierce the thick hide of a bolting deer, or at least make the tourists believe it could. It was sharp and shaped well, but the edge could be honed more finely. He kept working at it, pressing. Working it until it was so sharp the edge would disappear.

The Mississippi ran spring high and muddy brown by his camp under the bridge. Cars wheeling between Minneapolis and St. Paul droned by on the interstate overhead. Tender spring leaves unfurled on the branches of the trees all around him. He sat on a square of limestone that had tumbled from the bluff above, the glass cupped in his right hand. It bit at the calluses on the heel of his thumb, but bloodlessly for the moment. The left hand worked the edge with the antler tine. He avoided the drunk camp upstream; he preferred this lonely spot looking east over the big river. *Gichi* meant big in the language his ancestors spoke, but what was river? *Zibii, ziibi*? A vague language memory. One was right. The sun was falling beyond the bluff behind him. Maybe tomorrow that job at the produce warehouse would come through. Cousin promised to put a good word in. Until then, dreamcatchers and glass arrowpoints. No handouts.

Knapping is what the anthropologists called this activity, flaking really at this point. His ancestors called it necessary. In a sense it was the same for him. Necessary. He'd tie it into the center of the dreamcatchers he sold to the Indian crafts store down on Franklin Avenue. Uncle told him that no one in the old days tied anything but a feather into a dreamcatcher's center, but tourists liked drama. That was what the point was about—stealthy enemies, huffing buffalo, bolting deer—so he always did it. He turned those bad ideas into something necessary. Food for a day, maybe a jar of coffee, too. They took care of him all right at the craft store. The drunks upstream depended on handouts, worked the on- and off-ramps of the interstate until they had just enough for a bottle. Tourists liked their pain—not feeling it, but recognizing it, cultivating it with their dimes and quarters. The drunks became what the tourists wanted. Forgetful. They hid their pain in the bottles scattered around their camp, and so he avoided it. He remembered. Forgetting was defeat. Tourists would rather forget their history.

He put a little pressure on the edge of the point, pushed the tip of the tine just there, firm and quick and a slim flake of glass jumped from the edge onto his hand. Then again. He thought of the flakes of chert on his great uncle's hand as he worked the stone into a point. When the old man died, he had taken the antler tine from the old coffee can Uncle kept such things in. The can in that shed out back. There was a lot of history in that bit of antler. Necessity. The death of a deer, nights and days at Uncle's, the memory of that house by the river. Nights so dark he would never forget, not like these city nights.

He bit another flake from the edge. The slivers of glass worked their way into the skin of his hand. The shards, these slivers of glass, suggested as many memories as the antler. Uncle, stone cupped in hand, tine at the edge. He pressed again and flake leapt from newly formed facet. He gripped it. Uncle had sometimes talked about the Catholic boarding school when he worked the edge. Fathers who weren't fathers. Brothers and Sisters who were neither. The filth of the language Uncle spoke with his grandmother washed away with soap. Strange words about God's love put in their place, but he knew Uncle only ever learned the wrong kind of love there. The priest's hand was a soft white thief on punishing cold nights.

The shards of glass dug painfully into his hand.

That school.

He didn't know it, but Uncle's words and hands shared it. The butt end of the glass drove the shards deeper as more flakes pressed from the edge. Droplets of blood welled from his palm now, and red streaks smeared the green glass. He'd wash that blood away in the river when he was done.

He pressed the tine against the edge and thought about Uncle running away from that school.

Uncle laughed quietly when he told the story; the bite of the tine suspended for a moment, and shook his head in wonder at his thirteen-year-old bravery. Snorted really, more than laughed, a tiny deer noise, a chuffing sound heard at the edge of the woods. Hunters in the old days turned toward such sounds, nocked their arrows, and drew their bowstrings back. The point sharpened for a merciful kill. Deer honored for their sacrifice.

Uncle dreamt of grandmother every night at the school, saw her nearly toothless face—her smile wide anyway—hankie dabbing at the spittle in the corners of her mouth, and one night ran toward that dream on deer legs. He saw her eyes smiling as she warmed his hands with hers, the damp touch of that hankie on his palm. Broth, warm on the stove; frost, chill at the windows; the river, slow in its course at the back of the house. The point driven home.

He made it as far as the train tracks. Only toothless dreams warmed him for the next week, punishing nights on a cold pallet in a shed behind the school. That chuff again, that shake of the head, the tine digging at the edge though now, still biting at the sharp memory.

The memory of those nights came back with the press of the point in his hand. The door opening. Father's hand on Uncle's shoulder, his touch a cold sliver of white light, his breath sour and hot in the cold room. The man's lips pressed hard against the soft part of the neck behind his ear. "It's not what a man does," he said. "It's what a Father does." Speaking to himself, whispering really, as he pressed harder. His breath coming in short gasps, rasping in Uncle's ear, still pressing harder, sharper, and the words he spoke turned to shards of glass in Uncle's mouth and when he swallowed them he bled. Slivers of his life bit away, the edges sharp with pain that never disappeared. "It's not what a man does," when the words returned. Spent words, but words edged with the fear of forgetting.

He pressed the tine against the edge, harder with the memory. Worked the point sharper, finding new facets in old pain. Working it, working it. Biting at it.

The blood from his hand made the green glass look gray in the fading light. Soon it would be too dark to work. He walked to the edge of the river and rinsed the point clean, then returned to the chunk of limestone and took a dreamcatcher from his backpack. He'd made the hoop of it from dogwood and wrapped it with red yarn. Grandmas in the old days would have used sinew dyed with bloodroot, but what did tourists know?

He took a length of unwaxed dental floss and wrapped it around the shoulder of the arrowpoint and tied it to the center of the dreamcatcher, and suspended the whole thing from the branch of a sapling. He looked through the center of it to the beach across the river. From the beach he looked up to the sky and into the indigo edge of the night coming in from the east.

The light woke him before dawn. Sharp on his eyes, the three-quarter moon beamed over the big river. *Gichi-zibii? Gichi-ziibi.* That was it. He remembered. *Ziibi* was river. And Uncle had called the moon *nookomis,* the same word he called his grandmother. A word they couldn't take away, that he never forgot. Her light touched the arrowpoint in the dream-catcher and shone brightly through the pain at the edges. Each facet there was a memory: Uncle, a damp hankie, the priest's pale breath, and his soft hands. The deer's sacrifice, the antler tine working the stone, the words they took away, and the words they couldn't. *Nookomis.* The smiling eyes of toothless grandmas. The moon. Her light filled the pain, burned through it, and bent it in new directions. Uncle never knew love. He could only share what he knew—pointmaking—all his knowledge edged with pain. He saw that in the moonlight and knew he had to remember. It's what a man does, he thought—then snorted. That chuffing sound Uncle made. The dreamcatcher was a circle, as was *nookomis.*

Dew on the greening leaves of early spring sparked with grandmo-therly light. He plucked a leaf from the dreamcatcher tree and cupped it in his hand. With a blade of long grass, he brushed the dew from all the leaves in his camp into the green cup, gathered all the light of it in his hand, and remembered all who had suffered and survived—Uncle, *ziibi,* the deer, the toothless grandmas, the moon—so he could live. He could not forget. He looked at the arrowpoint in the center of the dreamcatcher, at all those facets refracting his grandmother's light and touching his hand so he could raise the leaf to his lips, taste the light shard memory of the dew, and drink down the pain.

"He" had to be Grandpa, Fiona thought, and his uncle in the story must really be Great-Grandpa Dewey. He went to one of those schools. He ran away, but he was never caught.

The letter said Dewey was fifteen when he ran away. The story said Uncle was thirteen when he tried to escape. Fiona hated to think about it, but had Great-Grandpa tried to run away at thirteen and been punished in that shed? Raped in the cold night, alone. It began to make sense why she didn't care for churches, and never would. Any God who gave loving grandma's cancer and let priests rape young boys was not worth her time.

Did Mom know about her grandpa, Dewey? About what happened to him? She must, Fiona thought. Maybe that's why we feel the same way about churches.

Eveningstar

Sun falls, men. Falls beyond trees. Falls to earth there, men, there, beyond them trees. Beyond the dead trees shaped into your houses, there, beyond your footsteps, the sun edges toward the other side, another earth. Speak softly, men. Night is another earth.

Trees gather cold shadows, men, there where you seek me. Every shadow, me—your dream of another earth. Silent footsteps under dark leaves. No noise, men, no city, no war, no dead trees. Your footprints absorbed by the sun's distant fall. Another earth rises.

There, you gesture. There, in cold shadow! You stub-finger point. See him, you holler, see him!

Me, you mean. You see me in cold tree shadow, men. Distant like men, far from the warmth of that other earth. Cold men dream of warm earth and find only shadow, only silence. Men call that shadow silence me. Me, men, me! Why? I am not the cold shadow of your distant dreams, men. I am not men.

Me? I am a warm star, men, shining above them trees, above that sun now as it falls, drawn by distant gravity to another earth. That silver light in the west, men. Me. I warm the edge of the approaching dark, gentle blue sky to burnt orange to dark purple to the warm, close silence of night. My footprint shines in the sky there, men. There is another earth. Men, tear your eyes from the shadows. Look up, men, find me. The evening star resists the pull of grave cold shadow.

Look up, men, up! Warm yourself to the night of another earth.

There, men, there!

Look!

Find me!

Perfect Night

One, two, third, men.

One, eight, thirty-one, men.

Eighty-seventh, sixteen, four, men.

Listen! You think me dumb in numbers, men, and count my counting wrong, but listen, men, and count as I do. Count as this world shows you, not as you believe.

One, two, ninety, a hundred and seventy-four, men, then a thousand million. Then a perfect night. Did you miss that, men? Did you miss the stars emerging in the darkening sky? First one, then ninety, then a thousand million, men. Mind the perfect stars, men, and count as the sky does. Mind it true!

One, eight, six hundred and one, three thousand and fourteen, men, then suddenly eight hundred, then suddenly sixty-three, then four, then none. See how I count the cold snowflakes as they fall one upon another, tumbling through winding winds, falling fast then slowing, men, then done. Then, men, they melt on the warm swamp. Ten, three, none. They melt there, men.

Hear the swamp, men! Mind what's warm there. The swamp tells you that what you count disappears.

Count stars, men, and the sun's light claims them at the pink dawn. What you count melts in the light. Count snowflakes, men, in that small snow squall, and see if you get any satisfaction. Count them and they're gone, men, claimed by the swamp that claims my footprints.

Count me not in numbers, men. Count me real!

Listen, men! Hear my voice? Do you hear me holler on the hilltop, men, hear the echo off the distant lakeshore? Then listen! Mind me! I am that star, that snow, that swamp! Listen!

Indians in Space, Episode Four: Dark Horizon

Robinson sat on a rock at the river's edge, watching the sun sink over the top of the bluff on the opposite shore, falling into the unseen horizon of another lonely night. A small fire blazed on the shore behind him.

His old lady kicked him out when his drinking got out of hand and he'd now spent six weeks living under a tarp by the river. The booze had dried up three days ago, but the hell of it was his head still ached and his tongue was still thick and woolly and he sometimes startled out of sleep gasping for breath. His days seemed numbered. She'd have him back if he straightened up, but the truth of it was he'd be back at the drink if he had five bucks.

He watched the muddy water of late summer swirling past in the last light. He thought it'd be nice to fill his pockets with rocks and just walk out into the Mississippi. The lights from the city would be swallowed as his eyes broke the dark horizon of the river's surface and he passed into the watery deep.

"Hell." Robinson threw a stone out into the river instead. "I'm such a coward." He'd never fill his pockets with rocks; he wanted to, so really there was no telling, maybe one day, but for now there was only "Hell" and another rock thrown. This one clanked though, stopped in midair, its arc interrupted, and then it dropped straight into the water with a plop.

"Hey," Robinson shouted. "Who's out there?" He jumped up and grabbed a flaming stick from the fire. "You can go ahead and leave," he shouted. "Or you can leave with your pants on fire!"

What he saw next startled him so thoroughly that he dropped the flaming stick into the river. It died with a sizzle.

Ten feet above the water a light appeared, illuminating nothing above but shining brightly on the water below. It seemed to Robinson as if an attic door had opened, only there was no ceiling in the middle of the river.

A being descended from the light, and another followed. Both beings stood on the water in the glow from above, each with an arm lifted in greeting.

"Angels," Robinson said.

"No." A voice drifted over the water. "Indians."

Robinson made the connection then and smiled. Everyone knew about the Indians. This was pretty cool, he thought. He shouted out to them, "You're the space Indians, huh?"

"Keep it quiet, would you friend?" The voice was hushed. "We just want to spend a quiet night by the water." The men were gliding over the river now and as they approached his camp, Robinson could hear the low hum of some unseen mechanism. "Just one night, before all the hoopla of our return hits." The men stepped onto the sandy bank. "Care if we join you?"

Robinson didn't know what to say. He ran his hand through his hair. Of course, he wanted to shout, but they'd asked for quiet. He swept his arm toward the fire, as if ushering them into the parlor of some grand estate. Idiot, he thought. Don't be such a fool. They're just men. Mellow out. He grinned widely—stupidly, he felt—as they sat on one of the logs by the fire.

"Why here?" he asked. "There's nice hotels ten minutes from here."

"Hotels don't have that." Wayne pointed with his chin across the water, to the place where the Minnesota River joined the Mississippi. "That's where my people came to be on this world." He smiled at Robinson. "It seemed fitting to camp here our first night back from the stars."

Robinson nodded.

Wayne looked at the man sitting across the fire from him and saw hunger there. "Why don't you get some food off the pony, Amos."

Amos nodded and disappeared into their craft. After talking with space Indians, Robinson was not at all surprised that their craft was invisible. He shook his head. Things at the river certainly could get strange.

"Hey," Robinson said, reaching into his backpack and pulling out a couple cans, "I've got some beans to add."

"Ah, *pidamaya*. We'll have a real feast right here."

Amos returned with a bag of dry meat and some other food in Tupperware. "Pemmican and wild rice," he explained to Robinson. "The food our ancestors carried with them on their journeys."

Robinson opened the cans of beans and set them on the embers at the edge of the fire. He'd eaten beans, lots of them, with his dad and with the families that cared for him as a child— quite often it had been all they could afford, but it was good food too. Summer barbeques and school picnics all came with servings of beans. Good memories of even hard times.

As the beans warmed, Robinson saw Wayne taking in his camp. The tarp, the ratty sleeping bag, the empty bottles. His cheeks burned.

"Been down on your luck I see."

Robinson just stared into the fire.

"That stuff's not good for you." Wayne nodded toward the empties.

"It killed my grandfather," Amos added.

Robinson's head snapped up and he fixed his eyes on Wayne. He didn't have to listen to this. "I haven't had a drop in days." He hoped to sound defiant.

"But you want a drop, don't you?"

Wayne's smile disarmed him, it was gentle, and that flash of anger he'd felt only a moment ago faded. Space Indians were smart. No more weak excuses. "I do. I think about it every day."

"Right now?"

Robinson nodded.

"Do you have any coffee," Wayne asked. "*Pezutasapa?*"

"*Makade-mashkikiwaaboo,*" Amos countered.

Robinson didn't know anything about fancy brand names. He pulled a jar of Folger's crystals from his backpack.

"That'll work." Wayne turned to Amos. "Get the pot and some of that water."

Amos jumped up and disappeared into the air above the edge of the river again.

Robinson noticed Wayne had emphasized *that* water. He looked a question at the older man but before he could say anything, Amos returned with three insulated plastic mugs emblazoned with the words "Grand Casino Mille Lacs," a blue enamelware coffee pot, and a flask of water. The pot reminded him of his dad. Spoons dissolved in that coffee Dewey made.

As he filled the pot, Wayne explained about the water. "It's the first water," he said. "Like my ancestors found over there." With a tip of his head he gestured again to the place where the two rivers met. "The source of a good life."

Condensation gathered on the pot as the water warmed, evaporated, and then the cap started to rattle as the water began to bubble.

Wayne spooned crystals into each mug and mixed in the boiling water. He handed Robinson one of the mugs. "We call it *pezutasapa* in Dakota. It means 'black medicine.'"

"*Makade-mashkikiwaaboo* means pretty much the same in Anishi-naabemowin," Amos added.

Robinson wondered what "coffee" meant. He didn't know the meaning of his own language. He had only words, and his words were black holes.

The men sat sipping and staring as the fire sputtered. Its coals pulsed in the cool air off the river.

"It's been four days, hasn't it?" Wayne asked after a while.

"Yeah."

"Four days?" Robinson asked, the coffee warming his belly.

"There's an old one out there, dying." Amos gestured to the sky. "Singing its last song."

What kind of old one? Robinson wondered, but kept the thought to himself.

The young man began to sing a song, tapping a rhythm against the log he sat on.

Robinson listened; when others sang he always just listened. He never felt music like others seemed to. Of course, he was always drinking when others were singing. He felt only drink then.

Wayne joined Amos when the song cycled back to the beginning. The words were strange to Robinson's ears. They were bent and distorted sounds more than words, long aching sounds that rose and were contrasted with sharp enthusiastic shouts. As the song cycled around again, Robinson found his foot tapping the rhythm, his head nodding. He'd never heard such music before. He forgot about drink as the song continued and found his voice joining Wayne's and Amos's, stumbling on colt's legs, but the sound filled him and the words came spilling out of his lungs, uncertain, but real. He set the empty mug down by the fire. He'd never been much for singing, but he was singing now.

Fiona shifted on the bed and leaning back against the headboard reread the last paragraph. She still couldn't hear her grandpa's voice in the words and hoped she might hear him singing if she tried again, but got nothing. She let the pages fall on her chest and closed her eyes.

The story talked about both Robinson and Dewey, her grandfather and great-grandfather. This story about the space Indians made suggestions about their lives. This one told her a bit about Great-Grandpa's strong coffee and it said her grandma had kicked Grandpa Robinson out because he drank too much—at least it did if her grandma was "his old lady," but Fiona couldn't imagine anyone calling Grandma Rose that. "My old lady" sounded like someone with a cigarette dangling from her lip and a bottle of beer in her hand, someone wearing trashy black pants that were too tight. Fiona tried to picture her grandma that way, in a splashy purple halter top, too, maybe, and with a big tattoo of a blood-red rose on her arm since her name was Rose. Fiona chuckled at the image. The pictures of Grandma on their walls, propped on the mantel, and the one in Mom's drawer all showed a woman at many different stages of her life, but always fashionably dressed. Fiona glanced at her dresser, at the picture of Grandma and Mom she'd made a frame for in fifth-grade art class. Grandma was always put together well, as was Mom, Fiona thought. Looking at her scruffy cutoffs and simple cotton T-shirt, she wondered if anyone would ever say that about her. She didn't really go for those "on trend" girly clothes. Too hard to shoot hoops if you dressed like a mannequin at the mall.

Grandma couldn't have been his old lady, she knew that for sure. She was too not trashy. Maybe he had other wives or girlfriends after he left, one of those trashy sorts, who probably drank more than he did. Maybe one of them kicked him out. Maybe he drank too much trying to forget what he'd done to his Rose and had ended up living a drunken hobo life, like the down-and-outers who camped out by the railroad tracks a few blocks from her house. Some nights she, Strep, and Dane went over there to spy on their drunken goings-on. They'd seen a few fights that way, heard lots of slurring laughter, but mostly just saw sad people slowly passing out—drunk off their asses, as Strep always said. She closed her eyes hard against this thought, afraid of the tears that were warmly rising. She'd never considered that those hobos might have grandchildren—a girl like her. Had never thought of her grandpa living a life like that. She took a deep breath and, counting to ten, forced the tears back.

He'd gotten better, she knew. Someone must have taught him to sing when he was camping at the river and it helped him. Someone like that space Indian must have told him to drink good, pure water and give up on the alcohol that killed his grandfather. Her grandpa must have listened.

She opened her eyes and stared at the little plastic stars she'd taped to the ceiling when she was in second grade, the ones that still glowed in the dark. "*Anang,*" she said remembering the word for star from Grandpa's Anishinaabe-mowin glossary. Her gaze drifted to the spaces between the stars.

Maybe that's why he liked camping at the river—it helped him remember whoever it was that helped him get better. He and Misaabe could eat their beans, drink their instant coffee, and sing to their hearts' content out there. Or maybe Grandpa just told that mutt his stories, filled her head with his dreams, practicing them until he decided to write them down. Maybe that's what made him better.

That's where the stories came from. The river, his camp there.

She held her arm up and looked at the wrist, recalling when she was so frustrated that she tried to break it, when Mom refused to tell her what tribe they were, where they were from. She still didn't know much. They were Anishinaabe, she knew now, but that meant little.

Sitting up, she grabbed her phone and punched in a search. Some wiki page told her that the "traditional homelands of the Anishinabe, the western half of the Great Lakes region, are heavily wooded and have a short growing season, long winters and poor soil, unsuited to large-scale agriculture. The Anishinabe therefore were hunter-gatherers who lived in harmony with the seasons and their land as a necessity." She skimmed through the page and then shut down that window of her browser. The wiki only offered facts—flat, drab, and dull. So they were Anishinaabe, so they came from the Great Lakes, so they lived in harmony with their land as a necessity. Misaabe told her as much, but with more love and worry and anger at the way everyone had grown away from that life. Misaabe's words told her more about where she came from than any facts, way more than her mom ever shared, too.

She took photos of the pages she'd just finished, then put them on the bottom of the stack of stories. Holding the stack against her knee, she tapped the edges of the pages until they all lined up, and started back in on her reading.

The Lost Child

"Hand it over, would you?" P.K. put his hand on Dewey's shoulder. "I won't keep it."

Dewey shrugged the hand off, ignored his friend, and kept working his way down the path. It paralleled one of the many small rivers that descended into Lake Superior. Fog rolling in off the lake grayed the pine trees around them into ghostly spires. They were almost there.

"Just let me see it then."

Dewey stopped and pulled the tooth from his pocket.

P.K. laughed. "Not that old rock, the coin." Dewey seemed so small against the backdrop of the trees; P.K. was a head taller than his friend. He tried not to look down on Dewey and always tried to position himself on a lower part of the path when they talked.

Dewey stared vacantly at P.K., his brown eyes no more expressive than acorns. He didn't seem to notice or care that P.K. was so much taller.

"It's not a rock," he said finally. "Look at it." The tooth was small and hard and had once been white; a child's tooth. Dewey knew it was hundreds of years old. It had little fissures that he had never seen in his own teeth. He believed that cracked things were old things. The old paint on his house was cracked, old tomatoes in the garden were always split, and fallen trees along the path were always cracked at the stump. "There's a kid buried over there." Dewey pointed across the river with his chin. He couldn't believe P.K. found some old coin more interesting than the tooth.

"Bah," P.K. scoffed. "You're crazy." No sooner had he said the words than he regretted them. "I don't mean crazy," he began, but Dewey hadn't seemed to notice. His attention was fixed on the stone in his hand. He examined it as if it were a clue from which he had deduced a whole life. P.K. found Dewey's fixation on the rock worrisome. "You think about that rock too much," he said. "Just let me see the coin."

Dewey couldn't help thinking about the tooth. It was so old; old enough that it came from the days when this world was still mostly all Indians. It must be their child lost in the earth down there by the lake. The thought always chilled Dewey. Alone like that seemed more like abandoned. As far as he was concerned the tooth was a memory and it would lead him to remember what others had forgotten. He put it back in his left pocket, while he retrieved the coin from his right one.

"Here," he said and handed it over. P.K.'s pinkie was withered and brown like a twig. It must have been crushed at some point. It remained extended when P.K. closed his hand, as if he were drinking tea from a delicate little cup.

P.K. smiled. "Thanks." He saw a whole other world in the little coin; it was small and brown with uneven edges, as if a mouse had nibbled them. A Roman emperor was pictured on the front and in his face P.K. read a completely new history for America.

When he had found it two days ago, the coin had seemed somehow familiar to Dewey, like something he had seen before or heard about. It called up the vague memory of a story, maybe one his dad used to tell.

Lord! I wanted to shout, but dared not. These Indians little tolerated my complaints. They had agreed to carry me over the big lake in their canoes, but each time I opened my mouth to speak, their stern looks conveyed their utter lack of regard for my thoughts. It would be at least two more weeks before we reached the village where I would undertake my mission. Until then I was at their mercy. I sat; they paddled. All day my thoughts on you, God. I wonder if you can hear me. If so, provide me a sign so that I might know I still remain in your regard. A cruciform cloud reaching from the center of the sky to the far horizon would affirm my faith, but a day without pestering flies creeping up the skirt of my cassock would be sufficient. As the flies are now under my collar and the sky is but one unbroken cloud, I doubt you are much listening.

You seem—seem, I emphasize, God forgive me—to have forgotten me, deserting me to these Indians. Here, I have to endure their impieties in silence so as not to offend them. Imagine Christ, to not offend them. They, whose every gesture is an offense to the ransom you paid for their souls with blood! I cannot even wear the hat of my station during the day for fear that those behind me in the canoe will take affront at having their view of this lake interrupted. By day I wear my nightcap, inverting the natural order of civil life, to conciliate these Indians. Perhaps that insult to propriety explains your silence toward me, Lord. I am your child, and ever will be, but it would please me if you understood that any deficiencies you record in my behavior are evidence of the hardships that I suffer gladly for your Glory. My nightcap is not worn to offend the divine eye, but to ameliorate the Indian's.

As they continued down the path, Dewey timed his steps to match the rhythm of the distant waves as they pounded the shore. In Indian they called the lake *gichigami*; he couldn't remember why they called it "Superior" in English. Superior sounded big, like it was more important. He reached in his pocket and rolled the tooth between his thumb and finger, warming it. Bigger, he knew, was not always more important.

Movement stimulated P.K.'s thoughts on the coin and he began to chatter about how history was all wrong. "This is the proof, you know. The Romans were here long before Columbus." P.K. held the coin at arm's length, as if it were a divining rod leading to some untapped well of knowledge. "Their ships were big enough to cross the ocean and they were always in search of new lands to conquer." P.K. looked at the prow of the ship pictured on the coin's back. "Hudson Bay leads to Superior if you follow the right rivers. Just a look at a map and you can see how easy it would be."

Dewey found P.K.'s habit of speaking with complete certainty annoying. P.K. also said that wasps were smarter than honeybees, that oil was dung from bacteria that lived deep in the earth, and that the tooth was a rock. Dewey knew that just because you could think of something didn't mean it was true. Sometimes he thought it would be nice to remember everything that ever happened to him. He could have this thought, but thinking it didn't make it so.

"When they reached Superior, they must have been astounded." P.K. crowded up against Dewey when the path narrowed. "They probably thought it was an ocean, until they tasted it. Fresh and colder than any water in their empire. The lake must have seemed like a whole other world."

Dewey was not annoyed with that thought. The lake was another world; one he had explored almost daily for as long as he could remember. It differed from the woods and the river, and was certainly different from the chores Robinson made him do. Though it sometimes chilled him, the air off the lake seemed to clear his head and the tang of pine in it reminded him of Christmas, no matter the time of year. He remembered blinking lights on the tree, green and red and gold, and listening to his dad tell stories about the old days. It seemed so long ago as he walked toward the swelling pulse of the lake. He hadn't seen his dad in years; he missed those old stories. He had trouble even recalling them.

"The Romans worked along the shore, trying to figure out where this other world went. They pushed west along the shore, all along Canada, past the Sleeping Giant, and imagine how excited they were when the shore bent south." P.K. had forgotten the coin; the story had outrun the fact that sparked it.

The path went up a small hill and when they topped it Dewey could see the rolling waves through the trees.

"They just kept heading along the shore, until"—the path ended at a rocky verge and the sound of the waves pressed on their ears. P.K. raised his voice so Dewey could hear him over the water—"until they landed here!"

Dewey looked down at the mouth of the river. It was only a few feet wide and on its far side there was a low cliff just like the one where he now stood. The beach at the mouth was low and flat; millions of rocks worn smooth by the action of the water.

On top of that other cliff in the middle of a small stand of birch was a large gray rock. It reminded Dewey of a sleeping dog. Bigger than any dog he'd ever seen, but still a dog. He had been leaning against it a few days earlier. P.K. had been telling him about how a falling comet created the lake in a massive explosion and he was idly scratching in the dirt, not listening, when he found the coin and under it the tooth. Since making these finds, Dewey had dug in that stand of birch every day. He wanted to find the child so he could give him a proper burial.

The dirt along the shore was so thin that rather than dig deep, he dug long. Trenches ran beneath the birch, crisscrossing each other. They had found nothing since that first day.

"Give it back now," he said to P.K.

P.K. reluctantly put the coin in Dewey's hand. He couldn't believe that Dewey hadn't found a little box to protect the coin. In a box it would be more like an artifact.

Dewey pocketed the coin and began to descend the cliff.

P.K. resumed his lecture. "They beached their boats here. Probably for repairs and to replenish their food supplies."

They reached the beach and began to cross to the dig site. P.K. rambled on about how the Romans would have used pine pitch to recaulk their ships, how they had built huge fires to boil down the pitch in bronze pots, and how they should be able to find evidence of these ancient fires—shards of broken Roman bronze or the olive branches they used to stir the pitch. "Olive trees aren't native to this part of the world. An ancient olive branch, along with our coin, would prove the Romans were here."

Dewey ignored P.K.'s tale and focused on the cliff ahead, his thoughts on the beach and the lake. For as long as he could remember, he had spent summers and spare moments after school down here searching for agates, climbing on the cliffs, and fishing the narrow channel where the river entered the lake. It seemed like P.K. was always with him. Summer was only a distant memory today and school had long since been put from his mind. Every day was Saturday down at the shore. The world and its troubles easily forgotten. Now was all that mattered; now was all fog and spiny fingers of birch at the top of the cliff; now was finding the lost child.

Lord, these Indians seem to have no compassion. They are unforgiving and stern when afloat, crude and unforgiving when ashore. I live everyday as a victim of their unsubtle mockery. I am wholly dependent upon them and though they should depend wholly on you, they do not.

They mock everything about me, God. Everything from the way the skirts of my cassock wick up the water that collects in the bottoms of their canoes to the unfortunate fact that my right leg is shorter than my left, causing me to list when I pick up a basket of goods on our portages. I watch at night as they act out my limp and they never tire of the humor that under heavy pack I lean to my shorter leg and with the exaggeration that seems their nature they walk in gimp-legged circles. They seem to imagine that when one leg is shorter than the other the unfortunate bearer of the mismatched limbs can do nothing but move in circles, and so they turn in ever-diminishing circles until they collapse in dizzy laughter.

Every evening is filled with such sport, talk and tales over the fire while we eat. Some of the men sit rigid and grim-faced while they eat, their heads erect and tilted a bit forward, their backs as straight as I aspire to, and fix their eyes on some point in the dirt on the other side of the fire. Then they disintegrate into fits of base laughter and I realize they are deriding how I sit as they paddle their canoes. I try to sit that way because Lord, as you well know, in founding our order, dear Ignatius stated in his "Rules of Modesty" that a good Jesuit should not turn his head "carelessly from side to side but only for some good reason, when it is necessary to do so." They ridicule my loyalty to this rule as often as they ridicule my limp.

With my head erect and tilted slightly forward, as good Ignatius fussed we should, there is naught to do each day but watch the water churn by under their paddles. I dared not look to one side or the other and it became a sport among the Indians to get me to look left or right, but I gave them little satisfaction as the reflection in the water seldom revealed any marvel that need distract me.

I look for you in that water, though, but I see only myself, framed in hazy blue if the sky is clear, haloed with clouds if the sky is beclouded, or wet to the bone if you have seen fit to bring rain to a world which seems nothing already but water. I look at the picture of this man in the water and I see the hollow gaze of someone who is little interested in his mission to this world. That is why he will look neither left nor right and why he sits silently when the Indians attempt to engage him to speak. One young woman sits nearby and tries to teach him new words each day, but he responds to little she says. He thinks always of you, God, and where you might have gone.

Sometimes they seem genuine in their desire to make me look up from my grim meditations, for in the water I have seen many wonders including a strangely twisted tree, shrunken and weathered and alone on a rocky outcropping, that looked as if it were ancient when the Magi set their gifts at your infant feet.

I see these things, dear Lord, without carelessly turning my head from side to side, abiding by the instructions Ignatius devised for us and yet surpassing them at the same time. I hope you understand that this happens not through willfulness, but through the mediation of the water you have seen fit to place around me. The water is a small miracle and it consoles me on this trying journey and in that, my Father, I feel you have not forgotten me. Though I wonder more with each day, is this journey carrying your Glory to these benighted souls or is it carrying me away from you?

P.K. helped Dewey roll the log across the mouth of the river. It was the huge kind of driftwood the big lake tossed up on shore and it became their bridge once they wedged it into a crevice at the base of the cliff. At the end of the day, they would drag it back onto the beach and hope the lake didn't reclaim it overnight.

Stepping across the log was slow work and Dewey slid his feet one behind the other while P.K. held it steady, then he did the same while P.K. shuffled across. They began to climb.

The rock of the cliff was cold under Dewey's hand and slick from fog. One fracture in the rock's face provided a handhold and another a toehold. He began to climb. Someone had told him these rocks were almost as old as the earth and the fractures where he placed his hands and feet proved it yet again: old things were cracked things. Age had cracked these rocks long before the child was buried. He worked his way up. Putting his hand in this cleft—the last one he'd need to reach the top—was like reaching back in time, touching the world as it was billions of years ago. There was just some crusty lichen in there. It crunched gently under his fingers, but with the earflaps on his cap up, he heard it as loud as the waves below. He pulled himself up to the top. The last few yellow leaves on the skinny-fingered branches rattled in the wind.

P.K. joined him and asked, "Where do we start today?"

The lines of their trenches made strange letters on the ground. Dewey tried to read them. They had tried digging east to west and north to south already; the trenches all crossed by the sleeping dog rock. "There," he decided and pointed at the westernmost birch. "We'll start there and dig back to the lake." West to east was worth a try. The Indians said they reached the land of the dead the land by walking a western-leading road and so it stood to reason that walking the road backwards might lead to the child.

Flat rocks were their trowels. Dewey had stacked a few along the edge of the cliff. They formed a small monument, like a trail marker. Cairns, his father had called them.

"Our cairn," he muttered.

"What?"

He handed a rock to P.K. and took one for himself. "A cairn shows we've been here."

P.K. took the rock, shook his head, and followed Dewey to the western edge of the birch. "You didn't tell Robinson, did you?"

Dewey didn't care for Robinson. He was the young man who took care of him these days, and had for as long as Dewey could remember. Robinson acted as if he were Dewey's dad sometimes. Just that morning he had made Dewey put the earflaps of his hunting cap down before he left.

"He doesn't know." Dewey's voice went hard. "I wouldn't tell him anything." Dewey took the south side of the tree and P.K. the north. "He just makes my food and keeps my clothes clean and takes me to the doctor." He dug his rock into the thin moss under the tree. The dirt below was rust-red and smelled like wet iron. "As long as I'm back for lunch, he'll leave us be."

P.K. stopped digging and looked at Dewey. That was a major speech for him. He wondered if his friend might be improving. The doctors said it wouldn't happen, but they weren't always right.

Dewey hunched over his trench, dragging his rock through the dirt. The red dirt where he knelt was working its way into his jeans.

"Just make sure you take the coin out of your pocket when you get back." P.K. pointed at Dewey's jeans. "Robinson's definitely going to wash those tonight," he joked.

Dewey laughed without looking up from the trench. Mirthless was the word for his laugh, P.K. thought. Dewey knew to laugh, but didn't know what was funny. Doctors said that was typical of his condition.

"If he finds the coin, he'll probably send it to the university and those eggheads will steal our glory." P.K. cared little for eggheads; he liked people who worked with their hands. He returned to digging. "They'll figure out some way to explain how the coin got here, ignoring the simple fact that a Roman was here and lost it. They'll say a seagull picked it up, flew halfway round the world, and dropped it here, probably because he was exhausted."

Dewey listened but said nothing; he was intent on his digging.

P.K. sat up on his knees and looked at Dewey. "Those eggheads and their theories." He shook his head. "They always try to make what's simple complicated." He wiped some dirt from his cheek. "It's so simple, though. The Romans beached their ships down there and made camp up here in the trees. Someone had a coin with them and dropped it." He bent to dig again. "End of story. Simple. But," he sat up again, finger raised to make a point, "it proves they were here."

Dewey knew it wasn't that simple. There were no Romans outside of P.K.'s mind. He was sure his dad had told him the real story, but he couldn't remember it. He wished he could. He felt like it had something to do with the child he needed to find.

I look up to you at night, to the sky, my eyes filling with stars, clouds, rain, and mosquitoes—whatever you have seen fit to place above me—while my head fills with thoughts of these Indians and their easy way with my emotions and their blunt manners which are so different from ours, and I wonder about the state of the people in this world.

Yesterday a man shat within the hearing of all in camp and one of the children forced air from between pursed lips, in evident parody of the wind breaking from this man's backside. Lord, they all laughed and then laughed harder when the man returned and playfully sought to cuff the boy's ears while the child danced just out of his reach. The man was young and limber and could have caught the child with just the slightest effort, but didn't. The two circled the camp at a run. The boy vaulted fallen trees while the man fell over them. The boy hurdled the embers of last night's fire while his elder tiptoed through them, his face contorting in a farce of pain. It finally ended with the boy's leap into the shallows where he splashed water on the smoldering moccasins of the man. Rather than chastising the boy for his rudeness, his elders laughed and shouted what could only be encouragement to the boy.

They took so much joy in this coarse sport that I began to wonder if the emptiness of this world, the vast reaches of water, sky, and forest, had actually made them mad. They acted like squirrels more than men, skittering about camp, chattering in their strange tongue. I found myself wondering whether these Indians were even human. Worse though, I found myself wanting to laugh at the antics of the boy and the man. They raised the spirits of their fellows and every moment all the day long became an occasion for joy. I found myself sneaking glances at the laughing people in the canoes to our right and left, wishing I might join them.

The hours passed rapidly, but Dewey dug slowly, searching each inch he scraped up, desperate for evidence of the child. The red dirt, wet and cold, numbed his fingers, but he persisted. The wind moved through the branches above his head. He could hear a voice there, rippling the leaves, but he couldn't understand it. He drove the tip of his stone hard into the ground and dragged it through the dirt.

P.K. shouted. "Look!"

Dewey's knees locked when he rushed to get up.

P.K. was working in his trench, clearing the dirt from around whatever he had found. Dewey thought it must be a bone. He got up more slowly. His knees worked this time.

"See." P.K. pointed into the trough.

There was no bone.

"See what?"

P.K. took a stick and used it to lever out a shard of metal that was about the size of his hand. "Bronze." He picked it up. "Two thousand years ago a Roman pot shattered here. They did that if the fire was too hot." He rubbed the dirt from it, the red slipping away to reveal a yellowish-brown. "Bronze," he repeated. "I knew it." He spit on it and rubbed the remaining dirt off onto his pants. "They were here!" He turned the shard over. Dewey saw the word "China" stamped on the back.

P.K. stood up and threw the scrap toward the lake as hard as he could. "God damn it," he shouted. As it disappeared over the edge of the cliff, he turned to face Dewey. "That sure was stupid," he said. "I should've checked it more carefully before shouting." P.K. grinned, mischief crowding out sheepishness. "Of course, maybe I should've held on to it. It might be all I needed to prove the Chinese were here first."

Following P.K.'s lead, Dewey smiled, though he wasn't sure why. The Chinese didn't write in English. The bronze proved nothing. His smile faded and he stared blankly at his friend.

P.K. saw that empty stare and his smile fell. Dewey was incapable of understanding even the simplest joke these days; he could only respond to practical direction. "Maybe we should dig a while longer, eh?"

Dewey nodded and returned to the trench he'd been working. As he dug, the rock dragging red cuts through the dirt, his head began to fill with images of Chinese and Romans, coins and teeth—and forgotten children—and these images ran headlong into the sound of the wind in the trees and the water in the lake, headlong into his rock striking the earth and P.K. muttering about ancient explorers and the artifacts he couldn't find, and all these sights and sounds swirled together until nothing was clear. His rock began to stick in the earth, as if hardening in cement, and he wanted to cry because nothing made sense anymore, but with that feeling his head cleared. He was not confused. If he cried it would be for the lost child. The hole was still empty, but when he pulled on the rock, it dragged through the dirt again.

After a hard day afloat, the vast swells of the lake rising against us, we beached at the mouth of a small river and prepared to make camp under a copse of birch above the rocky shore. The soughing of the wind through the green leaves was just perceptible above the roll of the water. The young woman who endeavored to teach me her language listened intently to this sound, her ear turned to the treetops. She shushed the chatter around her with an emphatic gesture of her hand. We all fell silent and looked to her expectantly.

"*Mii-amaa*," she said and pointed into the trees. "*Bizindamok.*"

The sound returned and a murmur of assent ran through the group. I heard nothing but the sound of the leaves rippling against one another. The sun had begun to sink behind us, the sky becoming an indigo well above, and then I heard it too. A child's heartbroken cry. Heartbreaking, I should say. As the sun fell and the lake softened into looking glass, the voice became more distinct. It sounded like an echo off the treetops. His call came from the trees around us.

The young woman bound into the forest, calling, "*Indayaa-omaa.*" The others followed, spreading into the trees, echoing her call.

I listened as the child's voice shifted in register, rising with pain and then quickly dropping to a moan, as if his suffering were soon to end. It was the loneliest sound I ever hope to hear. Lonely, lost. I began to feel chagrined for thinking my days were rough. They were nothing compared to the night this child was entering.

Though I was unable to understand what the Indians were saying, their intent was clear. "Where are you?" they called. "Tell us!" They worked the woods, just as they did when stalking game, their expertise in divining a whole animal from the slightest spoor put to use in the gravest hunt imaginable.

One of the men shouted at me, his face severe. Though I did not know what he said, his words crackled in my ear with clear meaning. "Make use of your legs," he was saying. "He needs our help."

I began to search among the trees, stumbling in the gathering dark. A light glimmered in the corner of my eye and I turned, but it was gone as quickly as it had appeared. The child's voice was now only weak moan, a lonesome sound at an unfathomable distance. A few more steps into the trees and the light shimmered again, this time to my left. Turning, I saw a warm patch of light drop down through the air until it was prone on the earth between two trees. The light shifted from yellow to brown and began to melt into the earth; the child's voice became indistinct, muffled as if filling with some choking substance. I thought of the moss and dirt all around this place. I rushed to the spot before the light faded and began to dig at the damp soil with my fingers. The earth I knew had filled him.

"Here," I called. "Hurry!"

One of the men joined me, then another, then the young woman who had first heard the voice.

The ground seemed warm from the light and it cooled as I dug at it, grew colder with each fistful of red earth I removed. Afterimages from the light distorted my vision and when I looked up from the earth at the men and woman digging with me, their bodies were veiled in a spectral light. I rubbed my eyes with the back of my hand. The light disappeared and with it went the men and the young woman, though their voices still sounded near. As my eyes filled again with the dark, their bodies rejoined their voices. They dug with grim concentration. Time was against us and soon others joined us, digging at the earth, desperate to release this child from his misery.

Dewey sat up on his knees. His trench snaked across the ground, around trees, and crossed the trenches that he and P.K. had dug earlier. P.K. had stopped digging and sat on a large rock, looking at Dewey.

"You know it's almost two o'clock, don't you?" P.K. had been saying as much for nearly an hour. "Robinson isn't going to like that you missed lunch."

P.K.'s words were like mosquitoes: ignored, they were less annoying. Dewey looked up at the birches. The tangle of trenches on the ground looked like the tangle of branches above. Yellow leaves rattled against one another, but the voice he'd heard earlier was gone. He looked back at the trenches; the child that had been there was gone as well. The tooth, he realized, was the problem. The child's voice was lost in the rattle of leaves because he had taken the tooth away. He smiled; that made sense. Tooth gone, child lost; he understood. He stood up.

"Let's get back before Robinson gets any madder."

Dewey pulled the tooth from his pocket and walked toward the center of the birch. The child was lost because of him; if he put the tooth back the child would return. The jumble of the trenches was now only a minor distraction. He knew right where he'd found the tooth. The sleeping dog rock. The trenches centered it in a star of red earth that drew him forward.

We dug in the earth until it was too dark to see, Lord.

Where was your light when we needed it?

We turned over the raw earth until our hands turned red as the dirt. Women cried, imagining their own children lost. Hair hanging loosely around their faces, men dug with grim determination.

My cap had fallen off I know not where and hair drooped in my eyes, damp from exertion. We spoke little in our labors. Occasionally, one of the men would look to see if I was at work, but I never disappointed them. Though his voice had faded, the child still spoke to me. In his voice I heard my own. If the child went unfound, no one would remember me.

The night wore on and one by one we collapsed in exhaustion. The last I remember was leaning back against a large rock.

I woke to the sound of labor. The Indians were filling the holes they had dug. I joined them in covering the trenches we had opened. God, but we were a somber group.

Most had returned to the beach and were packing the canoes when I saw one of the old men standing next to the rock where I had slept. In the daylight the rock looked like a sleeping dog or wolf. The old man had his offering in hand, gesturing to the sun, and speaking the words I had heard every morning of this journey, but had never heeded. *Indasemaaka ji-miigwechiwitaagoziyaan.* He set the tobacco down by the east side of the rock and left to help the others load the canoes.

I returned to the rock and thought to make a prayer. Latin seemed an inappropriate language with which to address a child without knowledge of that language, and what could I say, dear Christ. Let this child rest? Give him peace? His mouth filled with dirt, his heart filled with fear, his spirit tangled in the branches of the trees. What did You have to offer him?

The water washed the rocks of the beach below. I thought about that old man and the tobacco he had placed here. I had none of their tobacco; I had nothing but some ink and paper and my rosary. Things that might have been anybody's. My mother had given me the rosary and the Abbot had made me a gift of the wooden lap desk I kept my paper and ink in. "Use it to share your thoughts with our Lord, Father Heroux," he said in presenting me the desk. The only personal vanity I had allowed on this journey, other than self-pity, was a small keepsake from my childhood in Rouen. A Roman coin I had found along the banks of the Seine. With it, I recalled home, friends, and the life I had left behind. It meant a whole other world to me. France, the past—a childhood playing along the river.

I took off my boot and shook the coin into my hand. I held it up to the sun and looked at the prow of the ship pictured on it. I tried to repeat what the old man had said but my tongue was thick and though

I could hear the words in my head, the sounds fell from my mouth like damp red earth.

Dewey knelt in the dirt by the rock and tried to remember the words his dad had always said when making offering. Syllables broke when he tried to say them, the words crumbling in his mouth like crackers, so that nothing came out but a tumbled rush of air. He didn't care. He pressed the tooth deep into the dirt.

I watched a tooth press up out of the dirt before me, wriggling up like a worm after the rain. I touched it and though I saw nothing, I felt someone's fingers press against my hand.

Dewey felt a hand on the other side of the tooth and suddenly he remembered everything. The Christmas lights again and his father's voice telling the old stories. His marriage to Rose and his father's death soon after; the birth of his son, Rose's face radiant with exertion, but serene, the child wrapped tightly in a blue blanket on her breast; leukemia, he recalled, and Rose was gone, her face again serene. Robinson going off to kindergarten and coming home from high school. He remembered all the years he'd left the boy behind, with other families, when he shipped out on the ore boats, remembered the house he and the boy had bought when he could no longer work. He recalled the first time he couldn't remember his way home and how he had covered his cold legs with fallen leaves and filled his mouth with moss to stave off the pangs of hunger, but ended up still hungry and spitting out the damp clods of dirt that clung to the moss. He remembered hearing a voice that night coming up out of the ground. It sounded like his father's. He knew why P.K. had to be with him and why Robinson worried all the time.

"Dad!" Robinson's voice cracked sharply behind him and Dewey snapped his body around to face the young man.

The hand had no sooner touched mine than it jerked away, a swift fish unbaiting a hook. Maybe it had been too much for me to expect a coherent sign, but I felt the warm press of the fingers even after they were gone.

It all ran away—the Christmas lights, his dad's stories, Rose, his son, his words. The young man was angry. "What were you thinking?" he kept asking, but Dewey didn't know. It was all gone. He looked at the spot where he had pressed the tooth into the ground and thought about that lonely child, lost without the tooth. What would his father have done to help him? He wasn't sure. He bent back over the little hole, pressed both hands into the dirt, and looked at it again and thought about what he could no longer remember.

He thought it might be a doorway to some other world. Father, he wanted to shout. Father, tell me what I can't remember. What this young man needs to hear. The words swelled in his head, threatened to turn to tears in his eyes, but his mouth remained empty.

I felt the hand again; it touched me where my own rested on the earth. The Indians were shouting for me to join them. I put my coin against the palm of that lost child and covered it over with a handful of dirt. "Let us remember this lost child," I said as I rose. Then I left my other world there with him.

His father spoke but the words were indistinct, as if his mouth were filled with dirt. He was trying to tell him those old stories. Dewey saw a hand in a black robe covering the coin with red earth, as if it were something his father had once told him. P.K. had joined Robinson and the two stood over Dewey. He looked up at them, suddenly remembering. "It belonged to him," he said as he took the coin from his pocket. "Our Father, a great-grandfather. Like dad used to say. That old priest."

My cap was still lost under the trees and I sat in the canoe, head bare to the blue sky, my cassock damp from the water splashing off the paddles. I thought about the lost child. If not real, what else could he have been. Was he a spirit? A memory? A dream we all shared? I was unsure, but I knew he had touched me more than God had.

The young woman who had first heard his voice sat in front of me. She turned and gestured to a massive rock cliff that rose above us. I craned my neck and marveled at this tower of granite, as massive as any cathedral in France, and then she directed my attention to the base of the cliff. The lake had opened a cave there, an enormous room we might have all fit within, canoes and all. The sun bounced off the rolling water, painting a swirl of pulsing light against the vault of the cave's ceiling. The young woman spoke and while I failed to comprehend the sounds she made, I knew from the fluid gestures of her hands that she was explaining to me the words by which I would know this light.

Her family's story was here. Dewey—and his Rose, the first Rose, her great-grandma. Grandpa Robinson. A priest. She was Heroux, just like Jimmy's letter said, a child of an Anishinaabe woman and that priest. Fiona Rose Heroux MacGowan. All those names inside of her, reaching back to gichigami—Lake Superior—and a river in France. Reaching up to some massive cliff towering over that water.

This is where we're from, she thought. These words and stories, the lake, the river, the water, at least in part. Both Mom and I. Grandpa's words can help her see that, see that she is more than a child abandoned by a man who didn't care. He cared, but not the way everyone else expected. He cared or he wouldn't have sent the box with these stories.

Fiona glanced at the letters from Jimmy and her grandpa on the bed. Setting the stories next to them while she got out her phone, she thought, They'll help Mom understand. She has to read them. It'll be good for her to learn what her dad went through, what her grandpa had endured; it'll be good for her to see what Grandpa Robinson wrote about. Even if the stories offered only a sideways glance at what really happened, Fiona thought, they'll give her a chance to see how he thought about things. Maybe it would all be as new to her as it was for Fiona.

A sudden upsetting thought flashed into her mind. What if it wasn't as new for her?

What if Mom had always known these things? Not the stories about the Indians in space and the Sasquatch, or any of the others of course, but the family details. Maybe she'd always known about her great-grandpa's dementia, what happened to him at that school, and how he left his son behind. Maybe she knew about Grandpa Robinson's childhood, how he was basically a foster child, if not an orphan, with a dead mother and a dad out on the ore boats all the time. Maybe Mom understood how lonely that could be, since her own father left. Maybe Mom knew if Grandpa had other wives and girlfriends after he left. Maybe he had other families, too, and that meant Fiona might have aunts, uncles, and cousins who looked like she and Mom did. Relatives she'd never met. Maybe they had family beyond the Grandma who died and the Grandpa who disappeared and maybe Mom knew everything, all about who he was and what he'd done. Knew everything and never shared it.

Scowling at the picture of her mom and grandma in that fifth-grade frame, Fiona saw how her grandma smiled warmly toward her, while Mom looked off to the side of the picture, her eyes glancing away from whoever took the picture. Even in photos Mom had that distant look, like she feared making eye contact with anyone.

She's known everything and just kept it from me, Fiona thought. Hid it away from me the way she hid that wedding picture for all these years. Never answering any questions, not because she couldn't, but because she was greedy. She didn't want to answer my questions—questions about our family, our lives—because she wanted everything for herself and her anger and her bitter feelings for the man who left her. All for herself. None for her daughter. For me.

Fiona felt sudden tears stinging her eyes and jammed the heels of her hands there and roughly rubbed them away.

My own grandfather and she gives me nothing. Nothing. Ever.

A disturbing feeling rose up inside Fiona, a harsh, glaring feeling—something she couldn't name, but that swelled with a dizzying white hum, swirling at her from a cold distance until it pushed away all thought, and all she could feel was anger and sadness and loneliness and knowing that Mom could tell her every-thing and told her nothing made that anger and sadness feel like betrayal, like something Mom was doing to her, like she wanted to do it—to keep Fiona out of it, but she wanted to be in it, needed to be. The tears began to sting through the hum and Fiona felt her nails digging into the heels of her hands, her fists clenched tight against the feeling as it filled her head, her fists pressed deep in her lap so she wouldn't smash her arm against the wall until the wrist broke. Mom wants to deny me everything and anything and turn it all to nothing.

Fiona felt herself collapsing through the feeling, falling through the hum toward the dark center of her chest, falling further into the feeling, farther from everything she knew, until she fell into something else, another feeling. She gasped—it hit her like cold water—and took a shuddering breath, drawing it deep inside.

She felt what Mom feared.

Her tears left warm tracks on her cheeks. She took another shuddering breath and looked at the picture of Grandma and Mom again, at Mom looking off to the side, avoiding eye contact. She held that breath a moment, let it fill her chest, then slowly let it slip out. The hum began to fade.

Mom was afraid.

Fiona felt that now—Mom's fear in those distant looks. Brushing the tears from her eyes, she understood how it all worked.

Mom knows everything about Grandpa, all that pain and loneliness in his childhood, even that lonely feeling of living out in the woods when he was doing that good thing of caring for his own dad. She probably knows he blamed himself for Grandma's cancer and that he drank too much and lived the life of a down-and-outer, even after he sobered up. She knows everything and keeps it all to herself, but she's not hiding it from me. She's trying to hide it from herself. She's afraid if she tells me anything about him and his life that she might begin to feel sorry for him and if she lets herself feel sorry for him her anger will disappear. She's told herself she has to be angry because of what he did to her and Grandma, and she's afraid of what she'll feel if she lets that go. She's afraid she'll feel guilty and afraid that she might have some other sorts of feeling for him. Love might be too strong a word, Fiona knew, but some sort of warmer feeling. Concern, maybe. Mom's afraid concern might grow into something like forgiveness if she actually talks about him and his life—if she actually tried to think about him as anything other than the man who left.

Mom keeps everything hid so she can avoid facing those other feelings and here I am thinking I need to hide these stories and letters from her.

Fiona shook her head against the last dim bit of the hum there. Hiding the stories was no better than her mom hiding her feelings.

Hiding the stories—and anything else, really—was a lie. Mom wished she was different from her dad, but all three of them—Mom, Grandpa, and Fiona—were the same. They were hiding things that should bring them together.

Fiona looked at the stack of stories on the bed and picked them up. He hid for years and years from Grandma and Mom, she thought, and then he died out in that swamp, but still wanted to share something with us. He asked Jimmy to pack them up and mail them off at the right time, because he wanted to share something with us, even if it's a handful of Anishinaabe words we've never heard and stories that really don't talk much about who we are. He sent them because he wanted to connect with me and he wanted to reach Mom as well, she thought. He wants to reach past her anger and sadness to see if those other feelings were there.

Fiona put the stories on her lap.

He missed her as much as he missed me, she thought.

Long Strides

Little one, come. Little one take hold. My hand to you. My words to you.
Touch my hand, hold them words. Listen!

Men seek what little ones hold. Men can't touch what they dream
to see. Men reach for me with plaster and inches. Men see trees but
scratch their chin with fingers. Men beat the ground flat, little one, my
homeground! Men don't listen.

Listen, little one, listen!

Little one, touch dreams, don't measure them. Walk with them. Leave
inches to men, leave beaten ground, leave men to scratch their chin.

Come! Step long, little one, step far.

Leave men, live tall.

Grandpa left everyone behind, but never stopped thinking about us. I am the
little one in the poem, but so is Mom—his other little one. He sent us both these
words, she thought. Words to hold like a giant's hand. Words that found her
after laying on a cabin's shelf for eighteen years. Words from a man who made
mistakes and who walked away into a swamp because he thought he was lost,
but he must've never been truly lost.

If he'd been truly lost Misaabe would've come to him. Instead, the giant
sent that little mutt with his name to remind Grandpa that someone out there
was still looking out for him. Mom kept that picture of him and Grandma for all
these years; holding on to it meant he would never be completely lost to her,
even after he died. Misaabe the dog helped him remember that others still cared
for him, like she did. Maybe that helped him write the stories.

After photographing it, she put the page on the bottom of the stack and saw
the title "Blackbird Coffee" staring up at her. She was back where she started,
with her grandpa at the mall. Strep had read it to her earlier and though she
could remember it perfectly well, she decided to read it again. She wanted to
try to sound out the unfamiliar words that Grandpa had said to the bird and see
if maybe she could finally hear his voice.

Blackbird Coffee

I don't speak Anishinaabemowin, the language of our Anishinaabe ancestors, but I know a few words and the words I know may once have made me invisible. On the other hand, it may have been bird magic that transformed me for those few seconds. Either way I disappeared. Here's what happened:

I went into one of those big suburban malls to get a jar of instant coffee at the dollar store. Inside the mall there was a blackbird darting from perch to perch above the courtyard, disoriented by the skylights that showed the outdoors while prohibiting it. Settled for a moment, the bird showed me its profile, glancing at me sidewise and yellow-eyed.

When I was a little boy, your great-grandfather had told me that if I wanted to communicate with deer, I had to speak to them in Anishinaabemowin, the language of the woodland. Recalling this as I looked at the bird, I manufactured something respectful—I hoped—out of the handful of words I was familiar with.

Trusting the creature's sharp senses, I looked up at him and spoke under my breath, "*Boozhoo, makade-mashkikiwaaboo.*" I hoped the black-feathered sky-surveyor would see the aptness in being addressed as the black hot liquid I mix up out of a jar.

Inspired by my attention;

startled by my ability to haltingly speak in a comprehensible language;

and/or offended by my words, the bird took wing and became liquid for a moment, a black dash across a white ceiling. Drawn by the blue earthlight dropping through the skyholes above, the bird sped into the deceptive glass and spilled to the floor twenty feet away.

With the words still warm in my mouth, I moved toward the fallen animal. Lifting the bird in my hands and stepping toward the exit I became immune to the stares of shoppers and window washers. No one could see me. Moments later I was outside, kneeling by a shrub near the entrance, the bird at rest in the shade.

A few days later I had a dream: I'm watching the security tape in a dark room. I see myself turn toward the sky, move my lips, take seven steps, and disappear.

PART THREE

Putting Out the Light

HIS EYES IN THE LAMPLIGHT WERE DIFFERENT THAN LAST SUMMER. FIONA knew things had changed for Chance since then, but they weren't empty, his eyes, like lots of people thought they should be. People like her mother thought crazy meant hollowed out, but Fiona saw it otherwise. Crazy didn't hollow someone out, even if the pills they gave the crazy did; instead, crazy filled you up. She saw something extra there in Chance's eyes, little silver flecks in the iris that made his pale blue eyes seem even paler.

Chance had been seeing and hearing things for a long time and what he saw and heard had filled him up, pressing against the insides of his head, always on the verge of pushing through. That was the breakdown, when it pushed through. That's why he had to go to the hospital, twice since March. He was out now, sitting on top of the picnic table in his backyard, smoking and talking, and then talking some more—and always smoking, lighting one cigarette off the butt of another. Pills slowed the race of his thoughts and made his tongue heavy, hard to shape around some words, but that didn't stop them, the words, and what he said about what he saw and heard had not changed much. Most of all, he was still talking about God and love like there was nothing else.

The kerosene lamp sat on the picnic table at the far end of the backyard, well away from the house, where the dark on a night like this was deepest. Strep and Dane had moved the table there earlier in the summer while she and Chance watched, putting it under the dismal spread of the little plum tree and its thorny limbs. They wanted to get a little distance between themselves and Chance and Dane's parents. Their conversations about life and religion were the kind that shouldn't be heard by anyone's parents because they were daring and unconcerned with what they'd been taught at home, at school, and in church.

Chance most often drove these conversations forward. He'd been a freshman at college when the breakdowns happened and all his friends had sort of abandoned him, and so, even though he was five years older than them, Fiona, Dane, and Strep had been keeping him company during these long summer evenings. Fiona knew that Dane did so mostly out of brotherly obligation, while Strep found Chance's reports on what the voices told him to be "trippy." Fiona thought so too, but while Strep would laugh at the odd things Chance might say—uncomfortably, Fiona thought, which meant really he was a little bit unnerved by what he heard—she found herself caring about things she hadn't really thought about before. She thought Chance very fragile; he was as delicate as the moths fluttering above their heads in the tangle of the plum's branches and his words were thin threads by which he tried to hold himself together.

Though she was sure he had never gone crazy, it seemed to her that Grandpa Robinson also tried to hold himself together with words. His stories told some kind of truth, even if they were not true.

She tried to tell the boys—Dane, Strep, and Chance—about this a few weeks ago. Strep knew about the box, knew it was from her grandfather, and asked about it when they all gathered at the picnic table the evening after it arrived. "So what did your old Pops have to say?" he asked.

"Your Pops?" Dane asked. Chance, just released from the hospital for the second time that summer, didn't seem much interested in anything other than shakily lighting another cigarette.

She filled them in on the box, how Strep had torn it open before she even got a chance to read the address label.

"Classic Strep," Dane laughed.

"A man is what a man is," Strep said, bowing. Then added, "But we all know Fee would've stood there for a half-hour wondering about it without opening it."

She laughed. It was true, and she knew it. "Yeah," she said. "All glory to Mr. Strepkowski for stealing my mail."

"I gave it back as soon as I saw what was inside."

"And that was . . . ?" Dane prompted.

"Words." Strep shook his head. "Pages and pages *and* more pages—all just words. More like homework than a gift."

"W-what sort of w-words?" When he was heavily medicated, Chance's voice sometimes quavered.

"Letters and stories," Fiona said, and then told the boys about the one from Jimmy describing how her grandpa had left him with the task of sending her the stories before he wandered off into the swamp on that long-ago cold January night.

"Man, what a way to go." Strep shook his head.

Dane played it cool. "It's not so bad. They say freezing to death is just like falling asleep."

Chance dragged on his cigarette and added, "He became swamp. We are always becoming something else all the time." He took another drag and his voice trembled. "N-now I'm smoke."

Strep looked from Chance to Fiona and smiled. He loved it when Chance said things like that.

Chance exhaled. "Now I'm not."

"So we know how he died. That doesn't answer the question though, Fee," Strep said. "What did the old man say to you? I saw the envelope addressed to 'The Grandchild.'"

"He told me a lot about his life, about his father, and things like that. Family stuff. Told me to never forget we're Anishinaabe." She did not wield the unfamiliar word well, had never heard it pronounced, but her grandpa's spirit was glad she tried to say it, she was sure of that. "He told me that our ancestors remember we're Anishinaabe, even if we don't always remember what that means." He hadn't actually said that, but Fiona had decided that was best way to sum up his words. She smiled. "He talked about his dog, Misaabe—a lot. He loved that dog. Even if she stunk."

"Is *Misaabe* an Indian word?" Chance wanted to know.

"Anishinaabe," Fiona corrected him, just as her grandfather had done to Jimmy. "Means 'Bigfoot.'"

Strep leaned his head back and yelled, "All right!" He whooped like the Bigfoot hunters did on TV when they were trying to contact the creature.

Dane snorted. "Fantasyland," was all he said.

"Bigfoot comes to you when you're lost," she explained. "My grandpa had written all these poems or story-things about him. Rants, more like. Misaabe is worried about people—how we live, what we think about, how we want to get to heaven, and he just thinks it's all a fantasy," she said shooting a glance at Dane. "He wants us to live like he does by paying attention to the trees and the rain and the stars. He says all we need to know about the world we can find by kneeling at a creek. 'Kneel there, not elsewhere,'" she said quoting her grandpa's words as best she could remember. "Not in church."

"We got it, Fee," Dane said. "It's not that hard to figure out."

"It's pagan," Chance said. "Paganism." He blew smoke at the mosquitoes that swarmed around his head. "God smites the pagans, bleeds them of the evil in their lives, even if it kills them. He loves them enough to sacrifice them. It's the only way to save them. The church is his knife on earth."

Fiona thought about telling the boys her grandpa's story about Father Heroux. If she understood it right, that priest had decided pagan was better than Christian, had become one of her ancestors, which meant he had given up his church—had decided it was better to kneel at a creek.

"Dude," Strep slapped the table, laughing. "Did you just call Fiona's grandpa pagan?"

"No," Chance said. "She did. I just told you why God kills pagans."

"Chance!" Dane bit the one syllable of his brother's name even shorter than it was. "Shut up. Her grandpa died and we don't need to hear any of your religious shit."

Chance drew a lungful of smoke and exhaled. "And in death he became something else, what God wanted him to be."

"I said give it a rest." Dane's voice was a low threat.

Since that evening Fiona had been reluctant to share any more about what her grandpa's words had helped her to think about. There were plenty of other things to think about, especially Chance's condition. He hadn't meant anything in calling her a pagan, because that was what he was really doing if he called her grandpa one.

She could forgive him those weird judgments he made. He was sick and what really intrigued her about him was not the inadvertent rude things he might say. What intrigued her was the question he had found in losing his mind. It was one that he worried over every evening, rambling through long digressions about finding new angles and perspectives, and telling them about distorted visions of things that lurked at the shadowy edges of normal life that wanted nothing more than to drive people away from what he always called love, but which seemed bigger than love because he spoke of it as a force that moved through everything, human or not. In many ways he spoke like Bigfoot, but she never told him that.

For Chance, love was everywhere. It was near and warm like the earth, cold and distant like the moon, and strange and ethereal like the darkness that stretched between them. He had breathed in the sweet aroma of the blossoms from the plum tree last spring, called it love, and declared that he was now a tree. "Love makes everything become something else," he said, but because his voice was so flat and his face so expressionless Fiona realized that love for him was not an emotional state or a physical feeling. His face never showed love, never warmed to a gentle glow, not even when he was filled with the perfume from those tiny blossoms. Love was the moon, cold and distant, a philosophical condition he considered from afar. He never touched anyone and stiffened if anyone touched him; there was no giving warmth in his sense of love.

Chance never stated his concern with love as a question, but Fiona knew it was a question about the darkness that surrounded everything and did it get in the way of love, of God. This darkness surrounded the moon in the sky, the lamp on the table, and each of them in their hearts, is what she gathered from his rambling thoughts. What was this darkness? That was what Chance wanted to know, though he couldn't ask it so simply. It seemed like the voices had other ideas and whenever he got close to what he wanted to say, they would begin speaking—saying she knew not what—and drive his words back inside. He just kind of folded into himself when that happened. She thought he looked so small then, like a timid little child. Those voices chastised him. The pills made them quieter, but it didn't make them go away.

Tonight he sat on top of the picnic table, his leg jittering so hard the table shook and he had trouble steadying the lighter at the tip of his cigarette. As the sky had started to fade, Dane raised the glass chimney of the lamp, borrowed his brother's lighter, and lit the wick. Black smoke curled from it as the kerosene ignited and their faces fluttered in the glow as the wick decided whether to stay lit or not. Dane tossed the lighter back to Chance and settled at the edge of where the light reached, his face lit intermittently as he checked his phone for messages.

Dane had grown hard this summer and quiet, kind of sour, Fiona thought. He only ever smiled when he got a zinger off, usually a putdown of Chance and his strange thoughts and the weird things he sometimes did. An image popped into her head from a few weeks back: It was Chance offering her a bowlful of peanuts soaked in soy sauce. Dane said, "Don't be an idiot; no one wants to eat crap like that," in that clipped manner he'd developed, talking quietly, through clenched jaws, but not even sparing his brother a glance. Dane stuck close to his brother, but rarely faced him.

Fiona found Dane's behavior both unappealing and attractive. His anger was ugly, but she thought she understood where it came from. The little brother had to be the big brother now and he resented it, hated the responsibility that no one had put on him, but that his mom and dad still expected. He didn't know how to be the older brother, he didn't know how to deal with the voices and give his brother some kind of relief, and not knowing had made him a little mean—but it made him attractive as well; somehow he needed something and she was drawn to his need. She wanted to lean back against him and let what was warm inside of her melt what had grown cold inside of him, but she couldn't allow herself to do that. They'd been friends since before kindergarten and so she couldn't even allow herself to say anything. Instead she found herself leaning toward the warmth from the lamp, gathering more heat should she need it. Dane just leaned toward the cold light from his phone.

Tonight was cooler than most and Strep, like Fiona, edged toward the lamp and cupped his hands around the base of it. "School's coming soon," he said, looking over the lamp at her. His round face rarely showed worry or anxiety or anything other than a kind of general amusement at the state of things around him; he was unflappable Fiona thought, exercising one of those eighth-grade vocab words that her teacher had said would come in handy someday. The exception to this rule—the only thing that made him flappable, if that was a word—was school. Most of the teachers at school called Strep "Mr. Strepkowski," but it was not stated with respect; it was uttered more in a state of fatigued resignation. As in: "Mr. Strepkowski would you please get back in your seat" or "Mr. Strepkowski put the chalk back" or the erasers or the teacher's chair or Sherry Rasmussen's hair binders. Strep had difficulty focusing in a classroom, had difficulty making good grades, and so many of the teachers wrote him off as a goof. What the teachers didn't see were the lengths to which he went to help his friends. He had taken the hair binders from Sherry Rasmussen's backpack because Fiona's hair kept falling into her eyes during class. Everyone at school knew this about Strep; everyone not getting paid, that is. Chance had told Strep at the end of last school year that he was smart about people, and teachers hated that because they didn't have a test for human relations.

Fiona looked at Strep's face in the yellow glow of the lamp. That scraggly peach fuzz on his upper lip might have been a shadow from the smoke if she didn't know it was what he called his "'stache." He'd opened the camera on his phone and was using it as a mirror. He stroked his fingers over his upper lip. "I was really thinking this would have come in a little thicker by now." He set the phone aside, pursed his lips, and tried to catch the reflection of the 'stache in the lamp glass. Fiona smiled. For being so thin and insignificant, that 'stache had certainly eaten up many hours of conversation, and consternation, over the past month.

A moth, fluttering towards Strep's face, caught Chance's eye. Fiona watched him watching it. It was his habit to take a quick drag on his cigarette and then rest his hand on his jittering knee for just a second before raising the butt and taking another quick drag. Time and again, Dane had told Chance if he'd lay off the coffee, he wouldn't be so jittery and so obsessed with his smokes, but Chance said it was the meds that made him twitchy. "Not the meds they give me for the voices," he told them, "but the meds they give me to control the side effects of the meds they give me for the voices." As Chance now tracked the moth's stuttering flight, Fiona noticed his cigarette was midway between his mouth and his knee, and the jittering had stopped for the moment, meds or no meds.

Strep still had his lips pursed and as the moth approached the lamp chimney, it rose up, drawn as moths are to the light, and got caught in the updraft of heat from the lamp and caught fire. It became a brief burst of white light, reminding Fiona of a delicate plum blossom, before it fell to ash.

"Whoa, did you catch that?" Strep asked, his 'stache forgotten for the moment. "That's what I call messed up."

"Poor thing," Fiona added.

"It's not poor," Chance stated flatly. "Moths can't be poor."

Fiona believed Chance when he said he felt love for the moon, but it surprised her that he couldn't feel it for a little moth. Maybe it's just too close, she thought. For someone like Chance, maybe love is best kept at a distance. Still she told him, "I mean it's sad that it died like that, so quickly."

"But it's something else now," Chance said. "It's not poor; it has died and entered the light." He nodded at the lamp.

"And the light killed it." Dane leaned forward into the lamp glow. "It's not alive; it's stupid. Brainless." Fiona wasn't sure if Dane was aiming this last word at the moth or his brother.

"Whether it was brainless, dumbful, or innocent, the light killed it and that's evil. The light is nothing to be entered." Chance took a drag and thought about his words. Light, Fiona knew from Sunday school, was supposed to be God. Chance seemed to be measuring that notion as he took another lungful of smoke. "Moths dying of light is evil and evil is the opposite of 'live,' just like the moth is now the opposite of alive." Chance leaned back but then rocked forward abruptly, pointing his cigarette at the lamp. "The light is evil, it's the problem. Light is not life; light kills. It's hungry and it pulled what was living in that little bug right out of its body and made it into a nobody, a no-body." He began to rock more steadily, gathering force, and Fiona knew he was moving through that building that he said was inside him, a building full of a thousand rooms, joined by short hallways that branched off in a thousand directions. Voices emerged from some of the rooms, Chance said, but he could never find their bodies if he looked for them. The voices were no-bodies.

Fiona could picture the building and what she saw was a hospital in the form of a maze, a cold and sterile place. She thought it must be dark there, too, lit always just ahead of wherever Chance happened to be in it, and he was always moving towards the light, but never quite reaching it. The halls and rooms of this dark hospital were filled to overflowing with cartons and boxes and wheelchairs and hospital gowns that obscured whatever it was that Chance needed to find. It was so cluttered that his thoughts were sometimes difficult to follow, but still he would talk and talk, winding his way down those halls and through those rooms, never staying in one place too long. Words tumbled out of his mouth as if every step in every room was a different thought. Dane told them that the shrinks called it derailing. "It means he's going off the fucking rails," Dane had sneered, but she didn't care what he thought because if she just listened, if she didn't try too hard to make sense of it, Fiona found herself understanding exactly what it was Chance meant.

"Switch off the light and turn on life," he said. "Don't you see? Unlit candles avoid moths. God doesn't live in light; God does not kill brainless moths because they're dumbful, God blows the dust back onto their wings when it rubs off on our hands. God loves moth life."

From the look on Strep's face, Fiona knew that somehow the word "trippy" would work its way into the conversation at some point this evening.

"God doesn't live in light. He lives in the dark, out there." Chance gestured at the yard beyond the table with his cigarette hand. "Churches sell light, sell candles, put everlasting candles burning bright on their altars white and they do it to kill God and the love that is God. God's a moth turned to ash in the church light."

He put his finger on some of the cigarette ash that had fallen on his knee. "This ash is God. Taste it." He touched it to his tongue delicately at first but then smeared it on hard, the way the priests did to the Catholic kids on Ash Wednesday. "It has none of the flavor of light. All the light went out of it when I tapped it loose from this little fire." He flicked the tip of his cigarette and the embers flared into tiny fireflies for a moment and then disappeared in the cool night air. "God is trapped in the light." He flicked sparks from his cigarette again. "God is love. A moth in the dark lives and in the light it dies, and takes love with it. I loved that moth." He stopped rocking. "I am that moth. You are that moth," he pointed his cigarette at Fiona. "We are all that moth, everyone everywhere is. The love we need is all around us." He wound the wick back into the lamp until it went out. Fiona thought the dark seemed darker as her eyes adjusted. "This is love," Chance declared. Fiona imagined him spreading his arms wide to show them all the darkness that engulfed them.

"This is not so warm," Strep muttered.

"This is bullshit," Dane grumbled through clenched teeth. Fiona could see, just barely as her eyes still hadn't fully adjusted to the love all around them, that Dane had pulled the chimney off the lamp again. "Give me your lighter, would you?"

Chance handed it over and Dane relit the wick. "You and your talk. It's all talk. Light, dark, love, God, cigarettes. You just jabber on about this shit or that shit and you never really go anywhere with it."

Fiona pictured Chance rambling through the halls of that building.

"But that's just it, little brother." Chance took his lighter from Dane and sparked his smoke back to life. "I know what to do for God tonight. I know what love he needs from us."

Strep leaned toward the lamp and opened his mouth; Fiona waited for the inevitable "trippy," but was disappointed.

"Dude," he said, his face avid in the light. "What can we do for God?"

Chance led the way, carrying a paper grocery bag crammed with some things he'd grabbed from the house before they left. "We're going to need them," was all he said when Dane asked what he had. "To the church," was all he said when Strep asked where they were going. "Ditch your phones in the house," he'd commanded before they left, and before any of them could protest he told them if they didn't the ritual would fail. "There can be no distractions when opening a door to love."

Strep limped as they cut through the bushes at the back of the yard and crossed old lady Willowby's driveway. (Fiona knew that the old lady would see their dusty footprints the next morning, curse them roundly, and then attack their tracks with her stiff bristle broom; she needed to erase everything that threatened her obsessive tidiness). "I'm handicapped without my phone," Strep joked when Fiona asked why he was limping, then brayed loudly as if he had an incoming text.

"Don't be a jackass," Dane said.

Strep pretended to read a message in the palm of his hand. "Shoot, it's just my mom telling me she loves me. Again." He stopped limping. "She only tells me that about eight times a day."

From the Willowby driveway they made their way to the street and on toward the church.

The church, Fiona knew, was the red brick Lutheran one whose two-story tall stained glass Jesus overlooked the state highway below it. It was only a few blocks away, a five- or ten-minute walk she'd made hundreds of times. The hill that the church stood atop was a favorite sledding spot. She, Dane, and Chance had gone to Sunday school there and it was where they learned their small catechism. Dane and Chance had also been confirmed there, but she hadn't been able to work her way through all the confirmation lessons because, frankly, it hadn't mattered all that much to her. The God she met at church struck her as a small-minded, and while others credited him with all manner of miracles and glories, she didn't see anything around her that needed his omnipotence to explain it. Oh, but look at the sunrise, some would say when she told them what she thought, or the delicate colors on a butterfly's wing. Feel the warm cheek of that little newborn there or breathe in the perfume of those beautiful blossoming flowers there, they would say in offering her proof of their faith. She didn't deny the beauty in the world, was willing to even to see it in a humble little moth lit up by kerosene heat, but the true glory in all these things lay not in their creation by someone who didn't exist, but in the simple fact that they lived. Life was omnipotent, it was everywhere, and it was never jealous.

She knew life was bigger than God. We all came out of the swamp at some point and up onto the land, just like her grandpa had written in his poems. Then we stood up, she thought, and took a look at how rich in life the world was, here on Earth, sure, but on all the Earths around all the suns throughout all the galaxies as well. Life was huge—bigger than any stained-glass Jesus—and it didn't ask us to worship it, it just asked us to live it. Her grandpa's poems—the Bigfoot revelations, is how she was starting to think of them—confirmed that her vision of the world was the one she'd been born to. In the poems, he had revealed that Bigfoot wasn't the monster shown on TV. Instead, she had begun to realize that Misaabe was a sojourner, as her grandpa seemed to have been, alive and afoot in the swamps where humans rarely walked. Bigfoot rejected the world of man and listened to the world as it was, alive, and for Fiona that meant he rejected churches and God and lived as everyone should, with his ear turned toward life.

A few days ago Fiona had slipped up in her effort to not say anything about what she was learning from her grandpa's writing. She had told the boys she thought life was bigger than God. "He's jealous, Fiona," Chance had responded. "He broaches no discord and Jesus may suffer the little children but God doesn't gladly suffer fools. Pagan fools talk the talk you talk." So she'd stopped talking that talk, just to appease Chance; but not talking didn't mean she abandoned what she knew her world was.

The four of them rounded the last corner and began walking up the hill to the church. The street leading to the church was a dead end, a fact that always made Fiona smile.

The stand of woods at the end of the block had paths in it that she, Dane, and Strep had followed for hours upon hours over the years, ever since they were old enough to sneak out of their neighborhood without getting too frightened. The paths led back to the creek and beyond the creek to the swamp. Tramps, the real hobos, not homeless people or runaways, but the men and women who had turned away from the life of backyards, churches, and children, who preferred living rough and sleeping on discarded mattresses and hunks of foam rubber, made their camps where the swamp edged up against the railroad embankment. While Dane and Strep still went up and spied on the people in the camp, ever since she realized her grandpa might have lived that way, Fiona had decided she no longer found it entertaining.

Walking up the hill, the church was to the right and across from it were the handful of houses that they always called Party Alley. Unlike their homes, these places peeled and leaned in varying states of disrepair, and were inhabited by mostly young men who drank and smoked and yelled along with the lyrics of the music that pounded out from their windows at all hours, but mostly those late at night. The party was never ending and the dudes from the houses there were rumored to have done all manner of idiotic and bullying things to those who came too near their properties; most of these things involved making their victims do ridiculous and demeaning things like drink from the dog dish, walk barefoot through dog crap, or in one case that was well-known at school, but never really confirmed, one kid was said to have been made to sleep all night in a dog kennel. Treating their victims like dogs seemed to be the favored punishment the dudes would mete out, either that or, Fiona thought, being treated like a dog was what the rumor-mongers feared the most.

Grass grew knee-high or didn't grow at all around the Party Alley houses, and beer bottles littered the yards or piled up on the steps in front of screen doors that hung cockeyed from half-broken hinges. As they edged past the houses, Fiona could hear, even this late in the summer, even on a weeknight like this, music and voices pulsing from the backyards in a drunken drone. Passing by the houses, Fiona recalled walking to Sunday school and seeing, on more than one occasion, a person or two or three lying in the deep grass, sleeping off the party from the night before. In the semi-perverted manner of the teen-aged boy that he was, Fiona knew that Strep sometimes waded through the grass and skirted the front and sides of the houses looking for panties that some girls stripped off when they got good and drunk and slipped away with some similarly beered-up dude. Red-hot, drunken passion was a way of life on Party Alley and it was among Fiona's greatest hopes, now that she thought about it, that they would complete Chance's mission before the night got that red hot and passionate across the way.

"What are we doing here anyway?" Dane asked as they crossed the parking lot toward the church.

Chance raised the brown paper bag and held it in front of Dane's face, as if to say, *Isn't it obvious?*, and as he did so, a voice came out of the dark from Party Alley. "Fucking kids, what're you doing over there?" The dude's voice sounded like he had a beer bottle in one hand and a hammer in the other and he wouldn't hesitate to throw either one at them.

"Let's scramble," Fiona said, even as she began to run.

"Move!" Dane pushed Chance ahead of him and Strep followed close on their heels.

Fiona could hear voices from the houses back there laughing as they scattered. Dane passed her, bolting for the church.

"Maybe the door'll be open," Dane called over his shoulder, but Fiona knew that was a vain hope. It was after ten on a Thursday night and all the Bible study and AA groups would've long since left. The windows above the doors revealed not the slightest glimmer of light. She knew that the giant Jesus on the highway side of the building would be lit, as it always was, offering its warm glow to weary travelers, but the building was otherwise as dark as love.

"This way," Chance ran past the parking lot entrance and toward the back of the building.

"The kitchen," Dane said, realizing where Chance was headed. The kitchen was at that end of the church basement. The window wells there were ringed with thick hedges and once you pressed through the thorny brush, the wells were big and deep. A good place to hide, Fiona thought as she caught up with Dane.

Dane pushed through the hedge where it butted up against the church, the branches snagging at his clothes, and jumped into the window well. Fiona, at his heels, did the same. The red brick of the building was warm where her hands touched it, but the cement of the window well was cool to the touch. The sun didn't really reach down into here for very long, if it did at all. Fiona half-expected to see her breath. Chance pressed through the bushes and handed her the grocery bag before jumping in, followed quickly by Strep.

The four of them crouched down, slowly managing to get their breathing back under control. They huddled in silence for a few moments. Fiona listened to the cars passing on the highway below and watched as a plane crossed the sky overhead, its little white light hurtling forward through the dark.

Chance spoke. "These windows get left open sometimes. They crack them to let the steam out." He was close enough that Fiona could feel him shaking. He said the shaking was a side effect of the pills, but she was shaking herself a little bit—a side effect of that adrenaline rush of fear. She didn't trust those party dudes and suspected that Chance was himself a little worried, and if he couldn't smoke, she knew he talked to take the edge off. "They leave them open," he repeated. "We've got to get inside. No one will think we're in there."

"Quiet," Dane said.

"We don't have much time." Chance couldn't stop. "I'll crawl in and you guys follow me. They sometimes forget to latch them."

"Going off the rails," Strep whispered to her.

"Keep quiet." Dane's voice had the low growl of a threat in it.

"I'll crawl in . . ."

Dane clapped his hand over his brother's mouth. "Quiet," he hissed.

Their silence thickened in the cool air of the window well. Minutes passed without the slightest hint of any kind of pursuit. We're no match for beer, tunes, and discarded panties, Fiona wanted to say, but didn't. Just because there was no hint of further pursuit, didn't mean those guys might not be out there. Still, enough time had passed. She rose quietly and peered through the tangle of the hedge's lowest branches.

"I don't see anyone," she reported after a moment. "I don't think they're coming."

"Man," Strep said. "I bet they didn't even chase us, and even if they had, they would've tipped over with the amount of beer they put away." He laughed. "What were we so scared of anyway?" Fiona sensed a bit of macho posturing in the question; Strep had jumped into the window well as quickly as the rest of them.

"So what're we doing here?" Dane asked his brother.

"We've got to get inside."

"Fiona said no one's coming."

"That's why we're here though, no one or not. To get inside, to get to the light and get inside it and put it out before any more moths are claimed." Chance's voice lacked the quaver he'd had since getting out of the hospital. "I care about God and the moths fluttering in the trees and beating their wings against our hearts and our eyes, and I care about the love they're looking for, and we need to save him, and those who are us, the moths, our moth-ers, by climbing inside the light in here." He touched the window. "Once the ritual is complete the God we moths love will be home in the dark." He pulled at the edge of the window, testing whether it was secured or not. "It's what we came to do." The window showed no sign of give and Chance moved to the next one.

Fiona asked, "What ritual?"

"The consecrated tools of his deliverance are there." He pointed to where the grocery bag was leaning in the corner. "The tools were consecrated when I placed them in the dark; they've been blessed by the love that moths find in the dark branches of little plum trees. Once inside, the ritual will emerge as I bring the tools of love out of this bag." He gave up on the second window. "The tree is in the bag," he said and it took Fiona a moment to realize that the bag was made from trees.

"This is crazy," Dane said.

"But you're here, little brother," Chance said. "You came, and these windows are locked. Why would you come if your window was locked? Open your window, brother, let us in, and because the windows here are barred to us, we'll have to go up." Chance heaved himself onto the edge of the window well. "Hand me the bag, Fiona."

"Now what?" Strep asked as Fiona picked up the bag by its handle. Her knuckle scraped against a flat piece of metal that seemed to fill most of the bag. She could hear what sounded like a box of wooden kitchen matches in there too. It wasn't that heavy either. She handed it to Chance.

"We go up, I said," Chance said as he pushed through the hedge. "Up and over the top."

"Everything's over the top with him these days," Dane muttered, but followed.

"Ever dutiful," Fiona said to him as she climbed out of the well.

"And so are we," Strep said.

Once past the hedge, they stuck close to the wall. The setting moon was on the other side of the building and it cast the shadow of the steeple along the edge of the parking lot, but what little light there was didn't reach into the deep shadow along the wall. Fiona began to believe what Chance had said about the darkness. The shadow there kept them safe from the eyes of the party dudes. "It must love us," she said under her breath.

They edged along the wall until they reached an inside corner, where the wall of the parking lot entry met the wall of the hallway that led to the sanctuary. The church's roof was long and gently sloped and the eaves were nearer the ground than a house's.

"We need to grab the gutter and pull ourselves up," Chance said. "Dane, you go first."

"Why?"

"Because you're the strongest and quickest. You might need to help pull me up."

"No," Dane said. "Why do we need to pull ourselves up?"

"Because that's the way in."

"There's a hole in the roof?" Strep asked, joking.

"No hole, but we can get in from the courtyard."

Fiona understood now. The church was built around a little courtyard full of decorative trees and plants; she'd always considered it the congregation's own little Eden. Once they dropped down into it, they could go through the doors there and get wherever it was that Chance was taking them.

"What if the doors there are locked?" Dane wasn't going to go along with this plan just because Chance said it was possible. Fiona was getting a little frustrated with the way Dane always questioned everything Chance said or did. "Oh, come on, Dane," she said. "Stop being such a dick."

"Yeah, Dick." Strep punched him on the arm. "I'm ready to go."

Chance ignored them and looked hard at his brother. "You never noticed, did you?"

Dane didn't know what to say. "Notice what?"

"What about you?" Chance turned to Fiona. "Did you ever notice?"

"What?"

"They didn't put locks on the courtyard doors." Chance handed Strep the bag and, jumping up, grabbed the gutter. "They didn't think anyone would ever climb over the roof." He struggled for a moment until his shoe found some purchase against the wall and then pulled himself over the gutter onto the roof. Lying on his belly, he leaned back down and said to Strep, "You can give me the bag now."

Strep boosted the bag up to Chance, then jumped for the gutter and pulled himself up. "I never broke into a church before," he said and started scrambling toward the peak. "Keep low," he whispered, a bit too loudly Fiona thought since she could hear him from the ground. "The party dudes could see us up here." Fiona watched Chance following Strep to the peak.

Dane was next, grabbing the gutter, and then up. He immediately tucked low and moved after his brother.

Fiona jumped, and then jumped again. Her fingers could barely touch the bottom of the gutter. She prided herself on her ability to match Dane and Strep in footraces and shooting hoops; proud to be a tomboy, in other words, but pride didn't make her taller. She barely reached to Strep's shoulder and was a head shorter than Dane. "Hey," she whispered fiercely, but the three kept moving; Strep had already disappeared over the peak. "Hey!" She risked a shout, quick but loud. She didn't want to be left out there alone.

Dane looked back at her.

"I can't reach."

He crabwalked back down the roof and as he jumped to the ground, Strep poked his head back over the peak. "One of the party dudes just turned on his front light," he warned.

"Hurry up," Dane said. He grabbed her by the waist, lifting as she jumped, and gave her the push she needed to reach the gutter. As his hands touched her, Fiona felt a warm shiver pass through her body and liked how it felt. She got up on the roof and looked back as Dane pulled himself up again. His touch had never felt like that before, and she wanted to let him know how it felt, that warmth. "Thanks," she said and put her hand on his arm. In the distant glow from Party Alley she saw him smile, just a bit. Pleased, she thought, something she'd not seen in him much this summer.

"Come on," Chance whispered from the peak.

"Stay low," Strep added. "I see someone out front over there."

"I can hear them," some dude over on Party Alley called out to his friends. "But I can't see the little shits."

She and Dane scrambled quickly up the roof, over the peak, and down the other side. The drop into the courtyard was a lot farther than she expected. A shrub broke her fall, tearing her shirt a bit.

"We're never going to be able to jump back up there," Strep said. He didn't sound worried or anything, Fiona thought; he was merely making an observation. Unflappable.

"We can get out at any door," Fiona told him. "They all have panic bars for emergencies. Just push them and they unlock."

Dane nodded in the gray light. "Getting out should be easier than getting in."

Chance pulled the courtyard door open and a wave of stale air reached out at them. More sterile, than stale, Fiona thought as she followed Chance and Strep into the building, but old as well. The church smelled like its elderly congregants—gray and worn and slightly antiseptic. Tired like them too, she was sure; tired of all the singing and mourning and blessing. I bet it just wants to sleep, she thought.

The hall off the courtyard was dim in the night, but Fiona knew every inch of it from all the years of Sunday school. If they went to the right, the hall led past a wall of photos of all the young people who'd been confirmed in the church over the years, including shots of Dane and Chance. From there, if they rounded the corner, bearing right, and heading up a half flight of steps they'd arrive in the narthex. The double doors there were always propped open, unless the church was in service, and through them you had a straight view of the altar.

Dane headed immediately to the right, assuming, Fiona guessed, that the ritual would take place in the sanctuary.

"The ritual takes us this way," Chance said, moving to the left.

"Dude, it's a lot darker that way," Strep said, and it was true. The windows opening on the courtyard to the left were not full length like they were here. Down there they were just a narrow band along the top of the wall. "You got a flashlight in that consecrated bag of yours?"

"It doesn't make sense to take the long way," Dane said, not exactly griping, but close enough.

Chance responded, "Protestations mean little as the ritual abides by its own demands, not to the ones of those who'd be so dumbful as to be slothful." Chance often exercised words that sounded like nonsense these days, using them off and on for a while before letting them drop. "Dumbful" had now been used for a third time tonight and it struck Fiona as an ugly duckling of a word. It was awkward sounding but in the flow of Chance's thoughts it made its own sense and sounded nearly biblical. His words were a proverb with stubby wings.

Dane turned back and joined them without snapping at Chance. Fiona touched his arm and leaned close. "You're good to listen," she said. "He needs that." It was too dark to see if he smiled that pleased way again, but Fiona was certain he had.

Chance pressed forward. "The dark will take us down these halls counterclockwise as the ritual wisely guides us. Light would break this dark wisdom and leave it lifeless." Strep followed him, mumbling about flashlights.

"Come on." Fiona took Dane's hand and pulled him along. "What's a few extra steps?" He followed grudgingly, his hand cool in hers.

This route was longer and would bring them to the back of the sanctuary, where they would emerge from behind the altar. Following Chance and Strep, Fiona pulled Dane forward into the dark and through the halls, bearing always to the left—counterclockwise as the ritual had guided them, though no one but Chance knew why. Fiona wondered if maybe they were unwinding the clock, moving back to the time before God was captured by the light, but then it struck her, as they rounded the last corner, that maybe this was the route Chance followed through the halls of the building that was trapped inside him, the building with a thousand rooms full of all those confusing voices. Maybe, she thought, they were only trying to unwind the clock to the time before the voices started to speak and if they completed this ritual, Chance would find the relief the medicine didn't give him. At the end of the hall, a dim light flickered through the open door of the sanctuary, dissolving the darkness they moved through.

"Do you think someone's there?" Strep whispered.

"No, it's just a candle," Dane said as if there were nothing to worry about, but still his hand slipped from hers and he moved to join his brother. Fiona understood why, but missed his touch.

"This is where the ritual will be executed," Chance said as they entered the sanctuary. The altar was draped in white cloths and on top of it were a vase of flowers and two candleholders with unlit candles—Fiona smiled, remembering Chance saying that unlit candles avoided moths, yet here the four of them were—and in the center of the altar was a thick white candle, capped with a brass crown through which the wick burned brightly. Fiona looked at it. In Sunday school, they always called it the Everlasting Light. After their long spell in the dark, its brightness felt almost like a threat. It cut at their eyes and suddenly they were visible.

"Kinda hurts." Strep nodded toward the candle.

"It should," Chance answered. "It's his pain." He leaned the bag against the back of the altar. "It's why we're here, but there are certain preparations to make before we execute the ritual."

Strep leaned in closer to the candle, inspecting it. Fiona wasn't surprised that he stroked the ends of his 'stache in the reflection of the brass crown. He asked, "Why do they leave it burning? Seems like a fire could start."

"'Thy Word is a Lamp to my feet, and a Light unto my path,'" Dane said.

Fiona and Strep looked at him. "Sounds like poetry," Fiona said, something she wouldn't have credited Dane with knowing, and felt again that gentle wave of warmth for him.

"Confirmation class," he explained. "It burns there to let you know that Jesus is the light of the world and that his word may waver, but it never goes out. The flame is the love with which he burned for us sinners."

Chance laid a silvery-looking platter on the altar behind the Everlasting Light. On it he placed a length of rope and a box of wooden matches. I knew it, Fiona thought.

"He is the eternal fire burning," Chance said, "but everything else they taught us was deceit. Not even intentional, they were just moths drawn to the light of those lies." He ran his hand over the cloths covering the altar. "His eternal light doesn't burn on this piece of wood that they killed. It burns within us." He picked up the box of matches. "In the dark of us, is where the fire burns. When it burns outside of us, it threatens to consume us like that moth." Chance handed the box to Dane. "I need you and Fiona to break the tips off all these matches."

Dane looked at the box in his hand. He started to say something, but then looked at Fiona. She shrugged her shoulders. "All of them?" he asked.

"What else?" Chance said, meaning "Of course." "Two piles. One of the sticks and one of the tips."

Dane emptied the box on the altar.

"Not here. On the floor," Chance directed. "And don't let them touch."

"The floor?"

"Each other." Chance shook his head, reminding Fiona of a frustrated parent explaining something rudimentary to a little child. "Tips ignite sticks. Don't let them touch."

"Should I help them?" Strep asked.

"No, you keep watch." Chance turned his back on Strep and continued his preparations. Without any firm direction as to what keeping watch meant, Strep began to wander around in the sanctuary, moving out into the darkness among the pews.

Fiona and Dane sat on the floor below the altar and began snapping the red heads of the matches off the wooden sticks, settling into a steady rhythm that soon found the entire box decapitated and placed in two carefully separated piles. Brushing the hair out of her eyes when she finished, Fiona caught a whiff of the sulfur from the match heads on her fingertips. She looked at Dane and knew his fingers smelled the same and wondered if the two of them would catch fire if she suddenly grabbed his hand. The idea made her smile, and she felt again that warm rush as if he had just touched her. Shyly, she lowered her head and looked down at the pile of matchsticks by her knee, willing him to reach for them, to touch her, even if accidentally. Her hair slipped from behind her ear as she lowered her chin and she looked up at him through the hair hanging in her eyes. Through that veil and in the dim flicker of the altar candle, Dane seemed softer than she'd seen him all summer, his edges smoothed away, as he gathered the tips in the cup of his right hand. Like counting stars on a perfect night, he seemed to find it restful. He didn't have to think about what they were doing, what Chance had led them to do, which was, after all, breaking into a church and undertaking some kind of yet-as-unknown ritual to set a God she didn't believe in free.

"Hey," Strep came rushing out of the dark at the back of the sanctuary. "I heard something."

Dane stood up. Fiona quickly swept the sticks into her hand and did the same.

"What'd you hear?" Chance asked, moving around the side of the altar.

"It sounded like someone trying to get in at one of the doors."

Chance joined them in front of the altar. The rope he'd brought was now tied in a hangman's noose. Fiona felt her eyes grow as wide as Strep's did; Dane seemed to not notice. "We'd better hurry," Chance said, slipping back behind the altar. "We *will* hurry, but it won't take long now. All the pieces are ready to be put in their places."

"What should I do with these?" Dane held out his handful of match tips.

"I don't care." Chance was picking up the Everlasting Light and moving it off to the side of the altar. "It's the matchsticks that matter." Fiona looked in her own hand.

He slid the platter to the center of the altar and placed the noose on top of it, spreading the hole of it wide open.

Strep looked at Fiona, his eyes still wide, and mouthed, "Trippy."

A rattling sound came dimly out of the dark at the other end of the sanctuary. Though distant, the sound was unmistakably that of a door being tested.

"Someone's out there," Dane said.

"They can't get in unless they come over the top like we did." Fiona thought Chance sounded confident, and with equal confidence, he turned to face her. "Fiona, come forward."

She stepped to the front of the altar and looked across it at him. His eyes were unfocused, looking past her into the dark of the sanctuary.

"Do you have the matchsticks?" he asked.

She nodded.

"Please put some in each hand and raise them, palms upward and hands open so God can see they hold no light." Chance raised his hands as he wanted her to and closed his eyes.

She shifted some of the sticks to her empty hand and started to raise them as directed, when Chance whispered fiercely, "Wait!"

She froze.

"Strep, tear the blooms off these flowers and get rid of them," he said pointing at the vase. "But make sure that they don't touch each other."

"All of them?" he asked, even as he began plucking the blossoms and tossing them on the floor.

Chance didn't answer; he just kept talking. "The matchsticks are stems and the blooms on those stems are full of light pulled from the sun." Chance continued, "They could ignite a candle if conditions were right, but scattered around they won't be able to gather energy from each other and undo the ritual."

As he spoke, he lifted the Everlasting Light and placed it in the center of the noose. "Raise your hands, Fiona, open them to the Divine Eye and let him see that we have neutered the light, and that we love him as he loves us." His voice had none of the agitation it so often had these days. His words rang with a conviction that almost soothed her and she realized, without even consciously thinking about it, that Chance had seen this scene already, had seen her thin frame standing before the altar, had seen it in one of the rooms inside his head. She had now become one of his hallucinations, and what was strange was that the thought didn't disturb her. Instead she felt stronger; she knew she was in that room to help him, not God.

Strep pulled the last bloom from the last stem and tossed it over by the baptismal font.

"Now sprinkle the stems of the matches over the altar, Fiona, sprinkle them over the noose, and around the Everlasting Light." The glow of the candle reflected in Chance's eyes, and Fiona began to let the sticks trickle from her hands, and as she did so a strange feeling began to move within her. The wavering light of the candle and the rhythm of Chance's voice had a kind of hypnotic effect on her. She found her eyes closing and, as they fell, the sound of the matchsticks falling became more distinct. She could hear them pushing through the air as they dropped.

"Think about the darkness you've made those matches into, about the love you've saved now that they will never be lit," Chance whispered across the altar to her, the breath of his words merging with the sound of the air moving around the falling matchsticks. "Think about all the moths claimed by the light," he told her, and images and sensations began to move through her head as the matchsticks tumbled from her hand. She saw moths beating their wings in the dark and plum blossoms falling from the tree in the spring, she saw Chance's pale eyes and felt Dane's warm touch. Every falling matchstick was another image and as they fell she felt herself filling with a new feeling, one she couldn't name.

"Think about love," Chance directed. "Think about the darkness of it."

Fiona thought of Dane as the sticks trickled out of her hands, and she felt life rising from the swamp that was inside her, lumbering out of the dark water that swirled there. The feeling was vast and shapeless, an elusive shadow. Try as she might she couldn't get a fix on it; it moved just at the edge of vision and though she couldn't see it, she felt it turning to warm tears in her eyes. It was looking for her; it knew what she needed, but it seemed to be moving away from her.

The last stick fell with a barely perceptible "tink" onto the platter and Chance blew out the Everlasting Light, plunging the sanctuary into a darkness as deep as that lumbering feeling. It was so dark she couldn't even see the silhouettes of her friends. A moment ago, she had felt every word Chance said deep inside herself and she'd let them fill her, but now, the spell broken, she was unsure how she felt. This darkness was just dark; it no longer felt like love.

"Holy shit," Strep muttered, then added, disbelief edging his voice, "Really? The Everlasting Light?"

The sound of that rattling door was louder in the dark, seemed closer.

"We'd better move," Dane said. Fiona heard him grab the empty bag and then run down the center aisle. Fiona, Strep, and Chance quickly followed. The dark seemed less deep now. She could make out gray shapes ahead of her; that gray rectangle was the double door that led out of the sanctuary, and that waist-high gray line she saw beyond the doorway, was the railing along the stairway that she would grab to make her way down to the lower hallway.

Scant moments later she was there, in the lower hallway. The pounding of her feet on the tiled floor was indistinguishable from the echo of the boys' feet as they ran ahead of her toward the windowless doors that stood under the red glow of the exit sign. As they neared them, they slowed, listening. At first they heard nothing, and Fiona watched the dim gray figure of Dane reach gently for the door, as if with just the tips of his fingers he might be able to sense if anyone was out there. As he touched the door, it exploded as what sounded like a hundred fists began to pound on it.

"We heard you running in there, you little fucks," a voice shouted through the door. "What're you doing in there anyway?"

Fiona heard a beer bottle tip over on the sidewalk with a clank and someone muttered, "Damn it."

"Party dudes," she whispered to the guys, giving voice to what everyone already knew.

"Yeah," another voice rose beyond the door. "You kids stealing that good church wine?" Fiona heard at least four people laugh dully at the lame joke.

"This way," Dane headed quietly down the hallway, past the door to the courtyard. He stopped when they were well away from any door. "Here's what we're going to do," he began. "There are three exits on this side of the building.

That one with the party dudes back there. And then there's one just up that way," he made a vague gesture that the gray light made all the more vague, but was in the general direction they had just been heading; it opened on the parking lot facing Party Alley. "Then there's the one on the other side of the sanctuary, that lets out on the highway side of the building."

Fiona knew each one from all her years of Sunday school.

"We're going to split up." Standard operating procedure, they called it. Sometimes the bums would spot Dane, Strep, and her spying on the hobo camp and give drunken chase, but the three of them always evaded capture by rushing off in two or three directions. Dane continued, "Strep, you and Chance are going to go out on the highway side and Fiona and I will head out that door back there." He nodded back to where they had just come from.

"Bro, that don't make much sense," Strep said. "You'll run right into them, no matter how surprised they might be, know what I'm saying?"

"But they won't be there when we run out."

Fiona knew the rest of the plan without even hearing it. "Yeah, we'll make a bunch of noise at that Party Alley door, and when they come running to head us off, you two will already be out on the highway side and Dane and I will head back there," she gestured to the doors where they'd just been, "and we'll slip out right behind them." She smiled. "They won't even see us."

"Why don't you just come with us?" Strep asked.

"I want to make sure that we distract them so you two can get away." Dane leaned in close to Strep and said, "Chance might slow you down some, but I know he'll follow you and you'll take care of him, right?"

Strep nodded.

The dudes took up pounding on the door again and yelling at them, but they were far enough away that Fiona couldn't make out what they were saying. Whatever it was, she was certain it wasn't all that eloquent.

"Then we'll meet back at the picnic table," Dane said.

"But you two will have farther to go."

"True, but we're also the fastest runners."

"I bet we'll even beat you there," Fiona added.

"Yeah, sure," Strep muttered. "Believe what you want."

Fiona laughed. She'd run so fast when they got out the door that the party dudes would feel a breeze on their necks as she rushed past, her feet moving so quickly that she would fly right past Strep's skepticism.

"What's next then?" Strep asked.

"You guys make your way to the exit there on the highway side. You remember where it is, Chance?" Fiona saw Dane put his hand on his brother's shoulder in the gray light of the hallway. The younger brother was becoming the older one again, taking charge now that the ritual was ended.

"If it's still there, I do."

Fiona could hear agitation edging back into Chance's voice. The voices in his head often made him doubt that he knew what he knew. He sounded like he needed a smoke.

"It's still there." Dane patted his shoulder. "Now go, and don't let them hear you. We'll give you a couple minutes and then we'll start pounding on the parking lot door."

As Strep and Chance moved off into the dark, Fiona headed down the hall to the parking lot door, Dane at her side.

"Which way should we go when we get out?" she asked him in a whisper. "To the highway side?" She thought having the building between them and Party Alley would be a bonus.

"That's what I was thinking," he said. "Then we can always leg it across the highway if they see us."

The strip mall there would offer plenty of hiding places if needed. They wouldn't beat the other guys back in that case, but avoiding the dudes was more important than any grief Strep might lob at them.

The dudes continued to pound on the doors and yell. There wasn't anything to do but listen to their noise.

"This is going to work like a charm," Dane whispered. "Do you think we've given them enough time to find the door?"

"It's hard to tell time in the dark," Fiona said. "Let's give them a minute more, in case Chance has slowed him up." If Chance got agitated he could get indecisive. Strep might be pushing him out the door right now, or Chance might have tried to double back to his brother, forcing Strep to drag him along. Giving them an extra minute was a good idea, she knew, but the truth of it was that she also didn't mind this time alone with Dane and that would be over when they got back to the picnic table. She glanced toward the sound of his breathing, and even though it was too dark to really see anything, she could tell he was looking towards her as well. Something in the way they thought about one another was shifting. The dark was deep around them and absorbed the sound of the party dudes and all she could hear was the sound of her breath and his.

In what seemed like no time at all Dane said, "It's time" and moved to the door. "I'll push it open a crack and then pull it shut like we're sneaking out one at a time," he said.

"Make sure it latches," she said but realized that made her sound frightened, so she quickly corrected herself. "Make sure it latches loudly so the dudes can hear it over their own monkey noise."

The dudes continued to rattle the door and shout at the other end of the hall.

"You head back there," Dane said, "and give me a whistle when it sounds like they've left."

Fiona scampered back toward the door. She heard Dane push the Party Alley door open and then pull it closed, loudly. She smiled. Then he did it again.

"Come on," she heard one of the party dudes shout. "They're sneaking out the other door."

She heard the bunch of them running and someone claiming, "I told you we should've staked out both doors," and then they were gone. All was quiet on the other side of the door.

Dane pulled the latch closed a third time and Fiona whistled low and no sooner had the sound faded than he was at her side.

"Ready?" he asked. Without waiting for an answer he eased the door open and they were out. A quick glance toward the other door confirmed for Fiona that none of the dudes had seen them. They were pounding on it as they had been pounding on this door a minute ago. Dane guided the door gently closed, but as they turned to run around the opposite side of the church the back of a huge shadow confronted them. A party dude was peeing against the side of the building. "What the—?" he grumbled semi-drunkenly as he heard their steps and turned halfway around. "You little shits," he said when he saw them.

"This way." Fiona started sprinting toward the woods at the end of the dead end street. It was their only option, even though it meant crossing the parking lot in plain sight of the dudes at the other door. She knew she and Dane could outrun them, and once they were in the woods, the dudes would be clueless as to where she and Dane had disappeared. The trees in the woods were thin and scrubby, but grew in thick tangles that she knew every inch of, every major path and minor trail.

"I'm with you," Dane said, his feet slapping the pavement in time with hers.

"Guys," the peeing dude yelled. Fiona risked a look back. He was still peeing. Thank goodness for all that beer, she thought. "Guys," he yelled again. "They're getting away." Fiona imagined him zipping up as he shouted this and laughed, then kicked her sprint a little higher. They were most of the way across the parking lot now and the rest of the dudes had only just caught sight of them.

As they hit the path entering the woods, Fiona plunged into the dark of it without missing a step and bolted down the path, Dane at her heels. Twenty yards in, she dodged down a side trail, then hooked back left after a dozen more strides and hit a second path. The first one led back behind Party Alley and this one toward the creek. The Party Alley path was closer to home, but the long way seemed wisest in the circumstances. As he was still at her heels, she knew Dane agreed.

She could hear the dudes yelling and if they knew any words besides "little," "shits," and "fuck," she didn't hear them. The dudes were falling behind already and their voices were just distant, vague sounds.

She and Dane were both breathing hard from the sprint, but it was exhilarating. The air filling her lungs pushed away all the adrenaline her fear had released. She slowed her pace. "I doubt they'll find us now," she whispered.

"Let's keep running till we make the creek," Dane said.

The moonlight through the scrub left the path mottled with shadow. They moved in and out of the dark as they loped toward the creek. This late in the summer the water was low and they easily skipped across the stones there, like they'd done dozens of times over the years. Once on the other side, Fiona bore left through the tall grass edging the creek and then turned inland toward the trees. Dane stayed close. On the far side of the swamp, in the completely opposite direction from the dudes, they could hear a train rumbling down the tracks.

"There goes the 10:05," Dane said and Fiona laughed. It was one of the jokes someone would make whenever a train was rolling by. No matter the time of day, the train was always "the 10:05."

"Heading for Dykesburg, I hear," Fiona responded. Whenever someone identified the 10:05 whoever heard them had to name a funny town for its destination. She could always get a nervous laugh from the guys with Dykesburg. She'd found there was nothing more fascinating, or strange, to a teenage boy than thinking about lesbians. "They have two more of everything," Strep liked to point out, emphasizing *everything* with a creepy leer that she knew would one day get him slapped.

As the sound of the train began to recede down the tracks, other noises began to emerge in the air around them, grunts and curses and occasional snips of laughter.

"Hobos?" Fiona wondered, thinking of the camps below the railroad embankment.

"I don't think so," Dane said. "It sounds like its coming from the other side of the creek. Back where we just came from."

As the trundling of the train fell fully away, Fiona heard the sound of branches snapping and one dude yelp, "Damn it," as if a twig had poked him in the eye.

"Let's hunker down back here," Dane pulled her by the hand off the trail and into a little thicket of scrubby trees, which wrapped around them in a protective wall. "We can sit here," he said as he settled on the ground, "until they give up. It's so dark back here, they'll never see us."

Fiona sat next to him and pulled her knees to her chest; it was starting to cool down and her thin T-shirt and shorts didn't offer much warmth. The earth beneath her seemed warm, and though they were in the swamp, this August had been so dry that the ground wasn't even wet. In the spring they'd have sunk to their ankles just getting back under these trees.

"Where are you hiding, little ones?" a voice called through the scrub. Fiona heard a hint of menace in the question masked, just barely, with that snotty kind of wheedling tone spoiled brats used when tattling on their classmates, like those brownnosers she found so contemptible.

"Yeah," came another voice, only this one was mocking. "Fee-fi-fo-fum, you little Englishmen."

Fiona leaned toward Dane. "That one guy sure is a genius comedian."

Dane snorted, but kept otherwise silent. Fiona saw the sense in that. She leaned back against the tree and hugged her knees closer.

The dudes didn't have much more to say anyway. For the next few minutes Fiona and Dane listened as they lurched and lumbered around on the other side of the creek, shaking the thin trees, trying to scare them out of hiding.

"Dudes must be thinking they're monsters," Dane whispered to her. "Like Sasquatches or something."

Fiona thought about her grandpa's poems. The Bigfoot revelations. She knew swamps like this are where the big ones lived.

She heard one of the dudes snap a dry limb off a fallen tree. He began to pound it on the trunks of the trees near him, hooting loudly and grunting gutturally, sending his voice rumbling through the scrub. Even on TV, they knew that was how Bigfoot communicated with his kin in the distance.

"Man, shut up," one dude said.

Another added, "Yeah, that's creepy."

Fiona heard the guy crack, "Call me Squatch" and then chuck the branch into the creek. Clearly, he'd seen the same TV shows she had. He knew that Sasquatches lived in twisted swamps like this one, but the dude seemed to think the big one was something she and Dane would fear. From her grandpa's letter, she knew there was nothing to fear. She had gathered from Grandpa's words that Misaabe only emerged from his contemplation of nature if someone was twisted around and needed to be set right. If you were lost, he would find you according to the letter. She had pictured the big one wearing a Smokey Bear hat when she read that. Funny that a bear in a hat came to her as an image of security.

For the next few minutes, they listened to the dudes tromping over the ground on the other shore and muttering to one another, until one of them slipped in the muck at the edge of the creek and they heard his foot splash in the water. "Son of a—," he spat. "My new Nikes." Fiona wanted to laugh, but resisted. The dudes were wearying of the chase, but they'd be back on it if they heard her.

"I'm outta here," the Nike dude said. "Let's get back to the girls."

"And the beer," the genius comedian threw in. "Can't get one without having the other."

The dudes stumbled off, making their way back to Party Alley, but hardly quietly. They stomped down the path, muttering the same handful of lame curses they'd been tossing around all evening. Occasionally one of them would shout something nonsensical and full of tough-guy posturing about what he'd do "the next time I see you little shits." In between the muttering and the shouts, Fiona swore she could hear the unlucky dude's shoe squishing.

Soon, it was silent, or mostly so. The dudes were gone, but there was a bit of noise coming from the hobo camp behind them, on the other side of the swamp. Fiona was surprised she could hear anything at all from that far away.

"We'd better lay low for a bit longer," Dane said. "Maybe one of them is waiting out there to ambush us."

Waiting was fine with her; that feeling that things had shifted between them was rising in her again. What she felt was near at hand, its shapeless form moving like a shadow through the trees. Unsure how to handle this feeling, she leaned toward Dane and whispered, "Maybe Bigfoot'll jump up and scare the crap out of them."

He chuckled, but too flatly Fiona thought, and then suddenly serious, asked her, "Do you think Strep got Chance back?" There was an edge of worry to his voice that the hard Dane she'd seen all summer would never have shown. No wonder he didn't laugh at her lame joke. "I mean you never know with that guy what's going to happen next."

"Strep?"

"My brother, Fiona." Dane's words were clipped, short and hard, back to how he'd been all summer, but he realized it. "I'm sorry. My brother is not too reliable these days. Maybe I should've gone with him."

"Well, Strep would never have outrun those guys." Fiona put her hand on his, touching him without even thinking about it. "You needed to be the one to do that. You did the right thing giving those two the easy way home."

"Yeah, but . . ."

"But, what?"

Dane shook his head and looked down at the ground. "He's my brother. He's my responsibility. I shouldn't have put that on Strep." He looked at her.

"Geez, Dane, you know he can handle Chance. If nothing else, Strep's twice as big as him; he could just pick him up tuck him under his arm like a football if he needs to." She put her hand on his arm. "You know it was the smartest way to get him out of there."

"I just never know what to do with him anymore." Dane looked at the ground in front of him, shaking his head slowly, gathering his thoughts together, then unleashed them. "He's just so damn weird, spouting off all this religious crap, lighting cigarette after cigarette, then looking up at the moon and thinking it's full of love, or that the darkness between us and it is, or whatever the hell it is he's going on about. I don't get what to do." He lowered his head for a moment and then looked at her and laughed in that humorless way. "Christ, Fiona, we broke into the church and just watched when he blew out the Everlasting Light. They call him crazy, but we all just stood there with our mouths open and let him do it. Maybe we're all as twisted up as he is."

"We're not." Fiona put her hand on his cheek and tilted his face toward hers, and that elusive feeling started to take shape under her palm. She wanted to tell him that they weren't twisted at all because love was here in the darkness, just as Chance said it would be, only it was between them, her and Dane, not the earth and moon. She wanted to say something about this, but didn't have the words, and knew she didn't need them. She put her lips against his, unsure of what it meant to kiss a friend, but sure as well that it was the right thing to do. He leaned into her and put his arm around her shoulders. The darkness reached into them.

She shifted and let him lower her to the warm earth, her hands on his shoulders now. He kissed her again and she drew him closer, thinking that the sulfur on their hands might burst with flame and scar them if they weren't careful, but she didn't really care, because this moment seemed infinite, like it could stretch out from this one point on earth to the moon and far into the night.

He slid his hand down her arm, leaving a cool track of light where he touched, and then kissed her again, only what had seemed tender a moment ago now shifted. He pressed his lips against hers, but hard enough that she could feel his teeth through them, and she didn't want to. He ran his hand over her chest, stroking at her roughly, and she turned her head to break the seal his mouth had on hers. "Stop," she gasped. He pressed against her harder and tried to find her mouth again, but every time he got close she thrashed away, until he brought his hands together on either side of her head and held her still, his mouth mindlessly seeking hers. She bucked him off with her hips and pushed him away from her, and sitting up, scooted back against the tree. "I told you to stop." He knelt there, looking at her blankly, saying nothing. "I don't want to do any of that other stuff," she said. Her voice fell to a betrayed hush and she added as if it were a secret, "I just wanted to kiss you."

He held her eyes for a moment longer, then lowered his head. Sadly maybe, or maybe just frustrated, she couldn't tell, but it felt like he was searching for something to say, but no words would come to him. Just tell me your sorry, she wanted to say. "Just say it," she whispered but before she could explain what she meant, he leapt up and bolted away, his quick steps disappearing into the thickest part of the swamp.

"Hey, don't leave me alone out here!" She scrambled out from the thicket and tried to figure out which way he had headed. The paths back into the swamp were tangled with scrub and since the moon was gone now she couldn't even see if any of the branches were shaking, marking where he might have plunged through them. "Dane!" she yelled. He had come back for her when she couldn't reach the gutter, but she heard nothing now.

"Don't leave me out here!" she called, but it seemed hopeless. Stay quiet and maybe you'll hear him, she thought.

The creek burbled behind her and beyond that she heard the distant buzz of cars on the highway. The sound of hobo song and clanking bottles came softly through the thick leaves of the swamp, and then she heard a deep grunt. It came from behind her, far back along the path where the dudes had disappeared.

"Probably just one of those jackasses," she muttered, hoping the sound of her own voice would ease an unquiet feeling that had begun to creep into her chest. Her pulse was rising. She should just go home, but she couldn't go back past Party Alley, especially if some of the dudes were waiting in ambush along the path. They must be. Who else would've grunted like that?

Heading through the swamp and out to the railroad tracks was the only other option, even if it meant skirting the hobo camp. She didn't see that she had much choice. It would be so much easier to handle this with another person. It was not good to get too nervous, even in a messed-up situation; nervousness led to stupidity. Count to ten, she thought and drew a deep breath. As she did the old ones came to mind. Her ancestors lived among the towering trees of the north woods and called the forest home; they lived with bears and wolves around them and they weren't afraid. Her grandpa's words had made that clear. She remembered that in them and took another breath. His words had also told about flying snakes that would swoop down from the tree crowns at night and glide among the trunks looking for wanderers in the dark. Hold a stick in front of you, he had advised, just above your head and when you feel a snake wrap around it, you can whip it away with a snap of the wrist—or beat it hard against the trunk of a tree, she thought.

She thought about those Indians back then again. "They would laugh at me if they saw me worrying like this," she murmured, even as she bent to pick up a stick that was as long as her arm. "But it can't hurt," she reasoned. She suspected the flying snakes were probably really just your own anxieties swirling around your head, but having a stick to beat them back was better than having nothing to use on them. Stick in hand, she stood still for a long moment, hoping to catch the sound of Dane back in the trees.

Once she filtered out the hobos and the highway it was so quiet. She heard the gentle brush of some night bird's wings flying overhead—and it amazed her that she could so easily tell the difference between an unseen bird and a never seen flying snake. The stick worked.

Delicate crackling noises came up from the ground all around her, the sound of little chipmunk feet moving over dried leaves. No chipmunk would be out at the same time as owls, she knew. So what was this sound? It had to be the earthworms her biology teacher talked about last year. That sound was the worms eating the fallen leaves, breaking them down into the dirt from which more trees would one day grow. She jumped up in the air, as the teacher had suggested, and when her feet hit the ground with a thump, even the vibration from her small body was enough to drive the worms back into the ground. Everything was silent for a second, until an answering thump sounded in the distance. An echo, maybe, except she was definitely sure it was the sound of someone bigger than her—or Dane. She wanted to pull into the ground but couldn't.

It was just a lone sound, but it began to fill her head as she wondered who had made it. What if it was a hobo or one of the guys from Party Alley? It could've been the peeing dude, or maybe the Nike dude was stilled pissed about his wet shoe. "I shouldn't be thinking like this," she whispered. I shouldn't be here by myself, either. She thought of calling out for Dane again, but whoever else was out there would hear her as well. She was much more alone than she wanted to be.

She heard another thump, closer this time, then another. Footsteps, and the sound of breaking branches. Someone or something was forcing its way through the scrub upstream from her, coming towards her. The sound of her own blood rose in her ears, coursing through the veins there, and it drowned out what was left of the silence around her. Not hearing the thump of those steps was worse than hearing them. She couldn't take it anymore, so she raised the stick, and bolted for the heart of the swamp, hoping that her feet would take her past the hobo camp and up onto the tracks. She ran without thought, plunging headlong into the scrub. The branches scratched at her skin, trying to grab her.

The dark was deeper the farther she ran, but she kept pushing ahead, deeper and deeper into the scrub, mindful only of the need to escape. She swore the footsteps were closing. She couldn't hear them over her own gasping breaths, but she could feel each thunderous step shake the ground beneath her feet. She risked a look back and saw only the bulk of a monstrous shadow through the tangle of tree branches. Was it a man? Something else? It loomed there as big as fear and as tall as the trees. Misaabe? She felt a scream rise in her throat, but bit it down. As she turned back to the path, her toe caught on the crook of an exposed root and she found herself falling, could see a chunk of rock there on the ground and as it started to fill her vision, as she fell toward it, she twisted her body, shifting to avoid the stone. As she did so, she found herself beginning to rise up into the trees. She passed through the tree crowns, the leaves brushing her body with delicate grace. The damp air the leaves breathed out touched her face softly and, drawing their moist air in, she felt a sense of calm enter her body. The leaves were green clouds filled with rain, just like Sasquatch—and her grandpa—had said. It felt good to just float through them.

She rose up out of the swamp into the night above it, the darkness wrapping around her until she couldn't even see herself. Her body disappeared in the darkness, became a formless shadow drifting in the night, and though her eyes couldn't even catch the briefest glimpse of it, she knew her body was there because her other senses were sharper than ever. The air she moved through rasped against her, sandpaper on soft skin, heightening her sensitivity. The heat of the fire at the hobo camp, though just a dim flicker in the distance, sent a warm flush across her body and she could feel the starlight prickling her face. Footsteps in the swamp, still there, still in motion, sounded like waves crashing on a not-so-distant shore, filling her head with a pulsing energy that threatened to carry her away to she knew not where.

The footsteps were beyond her now and she could see the vast shadow that had been tracking her spreading over the trees beneath her until they were utterly dark and from the center of the darkness came the sound of voices crying out, but their words were drowning in the crashing roar of big waves. The center of that black hole began to shift, the night there began to twist, swirling into a whirlpool, and then suddenly a gap opened and she could see a night through it just like hers only someplace else. Moonlight shone there, though the moon had long since set here, and it put a silvery sheen on that other darkness. The silver darkness crowned like an infant pressing out from its world into hers and the gap widened, spreading open, and through it she could see what she knew were old-time Indians though they looked like nothing she'd seen in storybooks. They were rushing through the forest looking for something, calling out in words that were strange to her, but not to her ancestors. The sound woke something in her blood and she understood what they were saying. A child was lost. They were looking for her, but no one knew who the child was.

I'm here, Fiona called to them but the words had no form now that her body had merged with the air and the night.

Listen, one of the women there said.

I'm here, but even Fiona found that the words sounded more like moans than language.

The woman's voice keened with desperation. Tell me where you are? She wanted so much to help.

Here! Here! Fiona opened her mouth and closed it, opened and closed it, but no comprehensible sounds took shape.

Still, they moved and she saw them all, men and women, and a fat white man dressed in a priest's robes, trying to track the words she couldn't speak. Find me, she groaned, and the priest turned toward the gap, toward her, and fell to his knees. Here, she tried again to shape the word. The priest began to dig at the earth, pulling up the raw red mud of it with his bare hands. *Ici*, he said and looked up once more into the space where her face would be had the darkness not swallowed it. *Ici!* he shouted as he put his hands back down into the earth. He dug grimly, trying to reach her, but she was adrift among the trees above him, and yet in her heightened state she was also in the earth below him and in the air around him. She was everything—and his hands weren't clawing at the earth, rather they were stroking it. She could feel his hands moving across her hair, comforting her, not with his beliefs or his God, but with his love.

"He's our grandfather," she murmured. It was the priest, the one who chose to kneel at the creek rather than in the church, just as her grandfather's words had predicted.

"What did you say?" a voice asked.

Her eyelids fluttered, moth wings in the dark, and she looked up into Dane's eyes. Her head hurt. She closed her eyes; even the dark hurt them. "I don't know what I said." Her head was cradled on his lap and he was stroking her hair. It felt nice.

"I think the bleeding stopped," he said. He was careful to avoid putting his hand anywhere near her left ear; she could feel the blood clammily matting her hair there.

She shifted so she was lying on her right ear, the back of her head against his stomach, and Dane's hand was still comforting her. She opened her eyes. That lumbering shadow that had been following her was moving away from them, its bulk stalking back into the dark part of the swamp where her grandpa said the creature lived. Then it was gone. She closed her eyes again and asked Dane if he had seen it too.

"What?" he asked.

"The giant, that shadow, it was just there," she pointed in its direction with a tip of the head. "I felt its footsteps shaking the earth."

"I didn't see anything, Fiona," Dane said. "But you hit your head really hard," he offered, his hand still stroking her hair, and she knew he was right. Maybe. Soothed, she drifted in and out of waking, but always aware of the gentle caress of his hand.

"I wish I hadn't," he finally said.

"Yeah," she mumbled. She knew he meant what he'd tried to do to her and strained to open her eyes. Her head really hurt, but she twisted her neck so she could look him in the face. "Don't ever be like that again."

He smoothed the hair away from her eyes and she knew that was as much of a promise as she could expect from a boy. She laid her head back down. "What time do you think it is?" she asked.

"You were out for a long time."

"Midnight?"

"Easily."

"I am going to be in so much trouble." She pushed herself up. "We better get back."

As she stood a jolt of light burst behind her eyes, she stumbled, and the dark fell all around her. She ended up on her knees, one hand on the ground kept her from cracking her head again.

"I think we better wait until you feel better," he said.

"Yeah." She didn't have many words now, her head was swirling, and all she could think to say was, "I'm cold." She lay down on the ground and drew into a tight ball with her arm curled under her head. Dane lay down as well, moved up against her back and put his arm around her.

I knew you'd come back for me, she said, or at least she thought she said it. She meant to say it, but her head was so fuzzy she wasn't really sure if she had. Maybe she just thought it, but it didn't matter. Lying there with him felt better than all the trouble she was going to be in when she got home. She knew everyone was going to want lots of answers, but she knew as well that no one would ask the right questions. Nothing about her grandfather and the stories she'd read. Nothing about Sasquatch, or those old-time Indians, or how she could understand their strange language. Nothing about love.

Fiona twined her fingers with Dane's and pulled them up under her chin. He was warm, of that she was certain, and that felt nice. Maybe I'll kiss you again someday, she said, or thought she said, or meant to say. She closed her eyes and sank back into the darkness with him, nice and warm.

PART FOUR

Opening a Door

You want to know if I can tell you anything about who rents P.O. Box 343 and if they still do. You think his name is Jimmy, huh?

I can't really talk about particular postal patrons to the general public. Even the sheriff would need a search warrant to get that kind of information out of me, and I'm married to one of his deputies, Ralph Kamminga. But I can tell you this, no one named Jimmy rents a P.O. box here. We have our share of Jimmys hereabouts, but one came in about six weeks ago who was a little different. As he doesn't have a P.O. box I guess I can tell you about him.

No, he wasn't young at all. No one would say that. He'd been around town for a couple years, but you'd only ever see him come into town from God-knows-where a few times a month. Always walking, his dog and him. He'd tie his dog to a post when he got to the grocer's, then he'd head in and stock up on his necessaries. I was behind him in line there once when he bought a loaf of bread, some cans of beans and soup, and two jars of instant coffee. A bag of dog food, too, of course. Jen over at Jacobson's—that's the hardware store—says he'd come by in the fall and buy a couple boxes of ammo for a thirty-ought-six. Sometimes he went to the public library and that dog just lay down and waited for him. People say he'd type searches into the computers there, an old-school two-finger typer. Someone not too familiar with this modern Internet age.

No one knew exactly where he lived. We all assumed, without really talking about it, that he lived out in the backwoods someplace, off a narrow gravel road, in a shack sided with tarpaper that had a privy out back. He didn't strike any of us as too well off, but we didn't know. He kept to himself and we respected that. He didn't pry into our business so we left him to his own. Like I said, he'd been around for two or three years before he ever even came in here. Like I said, too, that was about six weeks ago, sometime in late July when he finally did.

"Yeah, *boozhoo*," he said as he poked his head around the door. "Dogs allowed in here?"

"As long as they mind themselves."

She was the scrawniest, muttiest-looking dog of indeterminate origin I'd ever seen. Terrier, dachshund, springer spaniel, Irish wolfhound—whatever was mixed up in her bloodstream didn't show up on the surface. She was just a hundred per cent "dog." Thigh-high on that tiny man and unique in all her own ways. The pup looked a bit like him too—it's kind of true what they say about pets and their owners. They were both skinny legged and watery-eyed. Her ribs showed through her coat, as I'm sure his ribs would if he took off his coat. Yeah, he was wearing a coat, even in the July heat. Old men up here do that—winter gets deep in their bones. The pup leaned against him as he stood there in the doorway. I always like a dog that's a leaner.

"Cute little mutt," I remarked. She smiled at me, used to hearing that word "mutt." "What's her name?"

"Niizh." He coughed as he said her name, and she craned her neck to look up at him, concerned in that way dogs are for their owners. "Damn these lungs. Sorry."

"Niizh, eh? That's an unusual name," I said. "Is it Indian?" I could see he was an Indian man, dark as he was. I don't judge, I'm just aware. Went to high school with lots of Indian kids. He might've been one of their grandfathers.

He told me *niizh* is how Anishinaabe say "two." "But her real name is Mi-sah-bay. She's the second little girl with that name, though, so I just call her Niizh."

"Gotcha," I said. I got it because we've had three dogs named Doris. This third one we just call D-3, like she was a rapper or something. Makes my husband laugh to say that. Not much rap music on his playlists, you know, but our nieces and nephews say we are so O.G. with a dog named D-3. I think they might be making fun of us, but it's all in a good teasing way so we let them.

By this time he had walked in his careful old man way up to the counter and put a brown paper bag on it. As he did so, Niizh sat and pressed up against him, like they were huddled for warmth, even though it must have been well into the eighties that day. She wanted to lessen that chill he felt. "What can I do you for, Mr. . . . um . . . ?" I started to ask, probing a little for his name.

He hesitated a moment, like he was trying to recall his own name. "Just call me Jimmy," he finally said as he pulled a stack of papers out of the bag. They were all held together with an old rubber binder. "What's the best way for these to get to the Cities?"

I handed him one of our prepaid boxes. "Anything you can squeeze in here goes for one price. The box'll keep them safer than an envelope."

He paid me with a wad of ones, then said, "Speaking of envelopes," and reached into the pocket of his coat and pulled out two letter-sized ones. He slid them under the rubber binder on top of the stack of papers, then asked if he could borrow a pen. He carefully wrote the address on the box in neat block letters. It surprised me, their neatness. He didn't look the type. Just goes to show. You know what they say about books and their covers.

No, he didn't copy the address from a piece of paper. He knew it by heart. Then he filled out the return address area. His hand tremored quite a bit as he scrawled the info there for some reason.

You develop a talent for reading upside down working on this side of the counter. I saw what he'd written as the return address and asked, "You have a P.O. box here, then, Jimmy?" I knew he didn't, but it's more polite to ask someone such a question than to just go ahead and say, "What? You don't have a P.O. box here."

"*Gah-ween*," he said. I knew enough Indian to know he'd just said no. "Just thought I'd put something down there," he told me. "If it comes back for some reason you'll hold it for me, won't you?"

"No, sir, I'm afraid I can't do that," I told him. His face showed a bit of dismay when I said that, but it turned to relief when I told him, "However, I can hold it for your little girl." I patted the front edge of the counter and Niizh detached herself from Jimmy's side and jumped up, putting her front paws where my hands had been, smiling ridiculously largely as I knuckled her right ear. No dog can resist the ear knuckle—three Dorises, one Brandy, and a Dutch had taught me that much. Niizh twisted her head toward my hand and sighed with pleasure as I knuckled in.

"Thanks," he said and smiled at me. "Niizh appreciates your kindness."

He recognized that it was a good tease from me, that I didn't mean anything mean by my little joke. It gave him a chance to see that I loved dogs as much as it seemed he did. Dogs never judge, like so many people do. So long as you feed them and love them, they accept you for who you are—all your faults, foibles, and fears are nothing compared to their love. They don't forget that love even if you might disappoint them every once in a while. That openheartedness is why I always say we have a lot to learn from the canine race.

After I finished with her ear, Niizh continued to stand there, just like a little kid next to her dad. She rested her chin between her paws on the countertop as Jimmy slid the stack of papers into the box and pressed the flap closed.

I did a quick check of the box before tossing it into the bin. I always do that check. You wouldn't believe how often people forget the most important part of the address, the zip code. That's the part that gets their message home.

Seeing that everything was in order, I told him with my best postal service protocol, "Fiona Heroux MacGowan should find this in her mailbox in two to three days." Then added, "That's quite a name to live up to. Makes her sound important."

Yes, I did say that to him. He smiled wistful-like and responded, "She is. She's the grandchild."

The way he said it made the word *the* sound like the most important word he'd ever say. "*The* grandchild," just like that. A whole world of pride and hope in that *the*.

"It's a gift for her, then?" I asked. "This box must hold your autobiography or something."

"No, just some stories."

"Family history?" I asked. I could tell he wanted to say more, he just needed prompting.

"Just little stories that might help her understand how we might see things." Niizh yipped inquisitively, just once, like she was encouraging him to say more as well. "Nothing she should believe, really, but yes, some kind of personal stories."

Niizh looked from one to the other of us and barked again, this time without any inquisitiveness, smiling eagerly after she did so, like she knew some great secret. She barked again, more quietly, more of a puffing sound really.

"She's a smart one, isn't she?" I could tell. Those attentive eyes and that conversational bark were sure signs that something was on her mind.

"That she is," Jimmy said. "Smarter than I ever was." He patted her as he moved toward the door and opened it. "She knows to stick close with the ones she loves. She never lets me out of her sight. I keep an eye on the ones I love, too, but hold myself at distance that she never does." She pressed against him as they stood again on the threshold, ready to leave. He turned to me and smiled in a sort of downhearted way. "I've only ever seen the grandchild in my mind's eye."

It was so sad the way he said it. His mind's eye. Can you imagine never seeing someone you love so much? He just slumped when he said it, too, like he was folding in on himself. The door closed then and he and Niizh were gone. I still see them come into town, but he hasn't stopped in again. Not even to check to make sure his package didn't get returned.

He was thinking about you so deeply that day, you know. You just have to be her, Fiona Heroux MacGowan, am I right? Calling and asking all these questions. Getting me to forsake the normal reticence my husband says I utterly lack. Ha-ha. Getting me to tell you anything at all about your grandfather.

So he's not your grandfather and you don't think he's named Jimmy. You say he's your father. Well, you fooled me a bit there. I was sure you were the grandchild.

If you're not Fiona, you must be her mother, I bet. Asking questions before she does, am I right? Trying to figure out what you should do now that she opened the box.

Let me tell you what I know, Ms. MacGowan.

It's this:

If you called, you must be as hungry for news about him as your little girl surely is. She's never even seen him, he said. I guess that means it's been years since you've seen him, too. You'll deny that interest, I'm sure—that's what family hurt leads us to do too often. And if you haven't seen him in years, you've been hurt. I'm equally sure though that you don't even believe your own denials at this point. The stories he sent raised that hurt again, but they also opened up something you thought you'd closed long ago. You wonder about him, are surprised he's still alive, curious to know why he did what he did. Why he sent that box. That's why you called.

You called, too, hoping I'd tell you to come up for a visit and tell you to bring that grandchild to see him. He longs so much to see her. I could tell he loved what he imagined her to be. He'd made her into one of those personal stories he said he wrote, but he wanted more than that I can assure you. He wanted to reach her with that box, wanted to tell her about himself and have her lean into him with a love like Niizh's. Unconditional, warm. I bet he wants the same from you, but doesn't know how to say it. So he speaks to the grandchild, tells her stories like a grandpa should.

So what if they're lies? So what if they're just stories he made up? It doesn't really matter. You don't even believe that really matters, do you? It's just your pride saying that. My grandpa told the biggest fish tales of anyone ever. Lies, for sure—but they were for me. They brought us together. When I was a little girl, I'd press against him when he told me about the muskie that spit in his eye when he was fishing and say, "That's not true, is it?" He'd put on the soberest face, as if I were judge and jury, and say, "As God is my witness, that fish could spit."

Your old dad is doing the same, but after so many years he doesn't know how to just sit down with you and the child and talk. He wants to or he'd never have sent that box. That's the way I see it. It's the way you should too.

I know he loves that little mutt of his and after his visit with me, I thought the only reason he kept on living was so he could take care of her. Now I know he was surviving for a dream as well. He hoped that box he sent would open some door to you and that little girl he'd lost in doing whatever it was that hurt you.

If that scrawny mutt wasn't with him and if he didn't have the hope with which he sent those words to your daughter, he probably would've long ago just faded into the earth and turned to dust. That's how he feels without your girl—and you too. Like dust. I can see that now in how he practically disintegrated when he told me he'd only ever seen Fiona in his mind's eye—he had done his best to imagine her, but that figment was no substitute for the warmth he had never felt.

Shuffling down Main toward the grocery store, Niizh, as ever, loyally in step, he saw that lady at the post office—Clara her name tag had read—chatting vigorously on the phone. He watched her through the window for a moment. From the way she gestured broadly, arched her eyebrows, and laughed, he knew she was enjoying herself. He suspected she always enjoyed herself; he'd seen that in her teasing manner when he posted the box all those weeks ago—and watching her now he was reminded of that. He smiled a little bit. He admired her joy.

Clara looked up at the window and grinned. For a moment his heart lifted. It had been so long since anyone had smiled at him with such warmth that he was tempted to cross the street and ask how her day was going. He knew she'd have plenty to say.

Her eyes were still on the window when he stepped out onto the pavement, but she was so deeply engaged in her call—still laughing and chattering away— that he realized she hadn't really seen him. Her eyes looked right past him to the car wash across the street. He was as invisible at that moment as he often believed he was.

He stepped back off the street and was about to turn toward the grocery store when he saw her half-extend her arm—acting out whatever story she was telling—and dig her knuckle in an imaginary dog's ear.

She's telling someone about when Niizh and I stopped there, he thought. He knew that someone had to be the grandchild. Who else would be interested enough to call? Who else would Clara be telling about his dog?

"Come on, Niizh, let's get to the store before she notices us." He turned and moved as quickly as his legs allowed, trying to get out of Clara's sightline.

If she saw him through the window, he knew she was the type who would rush out the door and drag him back to the phone, pulling him by the arm and telling him, "Yep, it's her. Your girl, and she's calling for you. You need to get in here and talk with her," she'd say as she pushed him through the door. "You've never heard her voice and she's never heard yours, but it's about time she did." She'd press the phone into his hand. "Speak, now," she'd order, a smile broadening under the high arch of her eyebrows. Clara would enjoy watching him stumble over the words as he tried to figure out what to say to a child he'd only ever imagined. Maybe he would, too—enjoy it, that is—but he also wasn't sure if he was ready for that conversation yet.

Niizh barked in that encouraging way she did when trying to coax him to open the dog food bag. "Stay out of it, you stinker," he scolded. "It's not happening today."

She barked again, wagging her tail.

Sure, he wanted to have that conversation some time, or he would never have sent the grandchild that package, but now was not the time, of that he was certain. It was not what he'd come to town for, not what he'd seen happening today. "Let's just get what we came for and get back home."

Niizh twisted her neck and looked up at him as they neared the store. "It'll happen," he told her, "but I don't know what I'd say over the phone." A phone call was not what he had anticipated when he sent the box.

Instead of a phone call, what he'd seen in his mind's eye was a car, like the shiny maroon sedan passing him now. It would roll past as he and Niizh neared the store, then would slow down and stop as a young girl bounced up and leaned over the back of the seat, pointing excitedly at him. Her mouth was moving, but he couldn't hear her since the car was sealed up tight against the dull August humidity. He knew what she was saying, though. "It's him, it's him." He knew the driver would shush the girl and try to get her to sit down, but she would refuse. "Back up, come on, back up!" The girl was pounding her open hand on the back of the seat, still bouncing excitedly, not listening at all. Even just thinking about it made him smile.

He could see the bright white in the taillights as the car reversed back to where he stood and by the time it pulled up next to him, the passenger window was already down and that little girl he'd dreamed of so often, the one who wasn't really so little anymore, who was at this point nearly a young woman, would reach through it and grab his hand. After all that time in the air-conditioned car, her fingers were kind of cold, but he felt them warming against his skin. She was smiling up at him and patting his hand, her face a beautiful reminder of his Rose, and his father's Rose, and of the girl's mother—and even of himself. He knew Niizh would jump up and put her paws on the open window, too. "Misaabe!" The girl would remember the mutt from the letter. "We found you!"

Leaning down to the window, he would smell the bright citrus burst of the grandchild's hair, see a bottle of diet cola in the cup holder between the seats and the driver's hand—thin, dark fingers like his own—resting on the shifter. The woman would look at him then and everything would change when she asked, "Dad, is that you?"

That night he had a dream. He was back at the mall, watching the security tape again, only this time it was running in reverse. He watched himself suddenly appear as if out of thin air in the middle of the floor with the blackbird in his hands. The him on tape was looking up to the skylights and though the camera was not angled towards them, he knew it was nighttime now, knew the stars and the moon pressed against the glass there. He watched as he lowered his head and with herky-jerky movements took seven steps backwards. Kneeling in reverse, he set the bird back on the cold tile floor. As he stood up, the little bird still prone at his feet, he watched his arms rise, saw himself smile as he turned into a young woman in shorts and a thin T-shirt—the girl in the car—and then with a powerful downward sweep of the arms he turned to bird, to wing, to flight and sped toward the warm light of the moon spilling down from above.

ACKNOWLEDGMENTS

I've had many enthusiastic supporters of my writing over the years. People who wondered if and when I would ever pull a book together and to all of them I owe great thanks.

Paul Udstrand and I have been friends for something like forty-five years and he changed the shape and direction of this book with a devilishly simple observation that clarified what I needed to do and why I needed to do it. Thomas King and Susan Power likewise encouraged me to rethink the early and middle parts of the book so as to bring greater depth to Fiona's ruminations and teenage emotions. I appreciate Paul's, Thomas's, and Susan's suggestions, as well as their persistent interest and support of my work, more than I can say.

Peace and love to my friend and intellectual mentor David W. Noble. His insights into the ironies of history and human experience shape much of the way I view the world and inform much of the way I write about it.

My parents, Keith and Ruthann Meland, gave me a good home full of books and reading that set me on my way as a writer. Their collections of poetry and leftist political tracts sat on a shelf under the TV and many were the nights I read my Yeats, Coleridge, and Blake or political commentary from people who wanted to end inequity, all while listening to Johnny Carson making wisecracks. I know this also shaped how I see and talk about the world. My vision of things would be so much narrower if Mom and Dad hadn't given me that space.

I have benefited from conversations about art, literature, American Indian writing, and Anishinaabe language and culture with too many students to name, but I want Em Wilson, Patti Sloan, Patrick Nylen, Beth Brown, Mary Barber, Cole Bauer, and Kaylen James to know that my mind is sharper and my understanding of writing and its relation to "this Indian stuff" is stronger because of what we've talked about.

My friends and colleagues in the Department of American Indian Studies have also been of inestimable support, particularly David Wilkins, Pat Albers, Rodrigo Sanchez-Chavarria, Brittany Anderson, Maria Littlewolf, Edna Day, Alex Ghebregzi, Miguel Vargas, and Carol Miller.

James Kaagegaabaw Vukelich helped me with the more complicated sorts of Anishinaabemowin that I use in the book and I have also learned much that I needed to know about Anishinaabe sacred law and cultural teachings from our many conversations.

James Autio is a fine poet and an outstanding artist. I can't thank him enough for his "Ahab," the crow on the cover of this book—the one who seems to be looking for something.

My friends at the Native American Literature Symposium have been an annual source of intellectual renewal. It's amazing what a few days in the company of other Native lit geeks can do for the spirit. I'm glad that talented writers and teachers like Gwen Westerman, LeAnne Howe, Heid Erdrich (who was the editor for my first published piece of fiction, "The Lost Child"), Molly McGlennen, and Jane Haladay tolerate my presence. Whether we're fishing, jawing, or eating, Joseph Bauerkemper and Ben Burgess are friends to the end.

Other friends have helped out, either by finding outlets for these stories, sharing stories that worked their way into this book, or just offering their kind interest: Judy Wilson and Steve Pacheco at *Yellow Medicine Review*; Diane Wilson and Jim Denomie; Pauline and Bob Danforth; and Avrom Schwartz and Elliot Schwartz have all been early readers and/or editors of these stories. David Range and Richard Range know what it really took to put out the light. Mike and Teri Welch share their schoolhouse with me. The poet Michael Kiesow Moore is the excellent curator of the Birchbark Books Reading Series here in Minneapolis. He graciously invited me to try out one of the stories in the book in front of an audience and then even more generously invited me back to share another one.

Gordon Henry, Julie Loehr, and the whole team at MSU Press have been amazingly supportive in shepherding this novice through the process of getting this book out. In particular, this book is deeply grateful to Gordon; it owes him its life. In October 2015, Gordon told me I needed to submit a book of essays to MSU—he's always enjoyed my essays—but being left-handed and slightly contrary by nature, I decided to send in a book of fiction instead, only I didn't really have one, but then a few months later all of a sudden I did. So the book and I say *chi-miigwech*, Gordon!

Miigwech Giinawaa! Thanks Everyone!

Some of the chapters in this book originally appeared in the following journals:

"The Lost Child" (Winter 2007) and "Blackbird Coffee" and "The Horse Chrysalis" (Spring 2012) originally appeared in much the same forms in the issues of *Yellow Medicine Review* noted in the parentheses. The four episodes of "Indians in Space" originally appeared in the Fall 2014 issue of *Yellow Medicine Review* in a slightly different form. The prose poems "Swampstep," "Bootfeet," "Swampbreath," and "Kneel There" appeared in the Fall 2015 issue *Yellow Medicine Review* under different titles and in slightly different forms.

"Working the Edge" originally appeared in *Lake: A Journal of Arts and Environment*, issue 7 (2012).

"Drunk Camp" originally appeared in *Fiddleblack* 19 (Summer 2015).